All about the Labrador

Portrait of Mrs Josephine Bowes and Bernadine, painted by Antoine Dury c. 1848. Probably the first portrait of a Yellow Labrador as we know it today.

All about
the Labrador

MARY ROSLIN-WILLIAMS

PELHAM BOOKS

Also by Mary Roslin-Williams
THE DUAL-PURPOSE LABRADOR

First published in Great Britain by
Pelham Books Ltd
27 Wrights Lane
London W8 5TZ
1975

© 1975, 1980 by Mary Roslin-Williams

SECOND EDITION MARCH 1980
Reprinted 1985, 1986

ISBN 0 7207 1218 1 2ND EDITION
(0 7207 0842 7 1ST EDITION)

Typeset by Granada Typesetting.
Printed and bound in Great Britain by
Butler & Tanner Ltd, Frome and London

Contents

Illustrations

Photographs

Line Drawings

Photo credits

Unless otherwise here acknowledged, photographs are by Anne
Roslin-Williams. The Bowes Museum supplied photographs
on p. **2** and p. **67;** Major Bruce Kinloch M. C., pp. **12, 114** *left*
and **116;** Gerard van Klaveren, p. **55;** Mr and Mrs Watts, p.
129.

Acknowledgements

This book is dedicated to Dr Keith Barnett M.A., Ph.D., B.Sc., M.R.C.V.S., who has done more towards the improvement of the Labrador breed than all the rest of us put together, with the grateful thanks of one Labrador breeder, whose Mansergh Kennel has depended for many years on his kind and sympathetic examination for the disease of P.R.A.

Preface

My aim in writing this book has been throughout to help complete novices, to answer some of their questions, and to advise them to the best of my ability on some of the daily problems, luckily usually very minor ones, that may arise with their Labradors.

I have tried to cover the major routine and general training of a Labrador from puppyhood right through to the time it becomes a 'made' adult dog. It is my sincere hope that it will help beginners to get the maximum possible enjoyment out of their Labradors, and I would like to think too that the more experienced breeders will also find something new to interest them.

It is also my hope that what I have said will help some of you at least in your quest for the perfect Labrador.

1 Buying Yourself a Labrador

The best place to start a book is at the very beginning, so although I fully realise that you may already own a Labrador or two, or even that you may be an established breeder, I am going to write at first for those who are only toying with the idea of getting a dog and who are considering the merits of various breeds to see what they would like to own, gradually working up to more advanced subjects as the book progresses.

There are many very good reasons why we breeders recommend a Labrador to newcomers and very few snags, all of which I will try and point out to you in due course.

Whether to Choose a Labrador

One of the greatest qualities of a Labrador is that they are happy, friendly, charming dogs, good-tempered, easily trainable, eager to please and devoted to their 'families' down to the very youngest member of the household. They will put up with almost anything from children and even get fond of the cat, if it treats the 'new boy' decently.

They are good companions to both men and women; good house-dogs who will give a warning if a stranger is at the door; good shooting dogs, the job for which they are bred; and they can be trained for all sorts of other useful jobs, from fetching the newspaper and your slippers to guiding the blind, and rescue-work from mountains and water. These tremendous qualities make them one of the most popular breeds in Britain, suiting practically everyone and able to fit in anywhere.

Another advantage of the Labrador is its cleanliness. They have short coats that dry easily and do not carry a lot of mud into the house. They are quick to learn their place and their routine (I shall suggest a routine in a later chapter on management) and are seldom a nuisance providing you are firm with them when they are young, taking a little trouble to teach them how they must behave and seeing that they obey you.

Being strongly and sensibly built without exaggerated and ridiculous fancy points, and with very few weaknesses in anatomy, they are very healthy dogs. They do not suffer from many cuts, bad injuries or broken bones, having thick coats, thick skins, and being well-padded

Major Kinloch's Logie Bhalu with a leopard cub. 'They will even get fond of the cat, if it treats the new boy decently.'

Logie Bhalu teaches the leopard how to swim.

with muscle. I find that apart from bills from my vet for inoculating my young puppies against distemper and hepatitis, I call the vet very little for ordinary minor accidents and injuries that other breeds sustain, such as rips and tears in their skin from barbed wire, torn ears, cuts, thorns and scratches. The heavy double coat, although short, seems to prevent these common injuries and mishaps, and the build stands up to bumps and knocks that would cripple a lighter-built, less well-padded dog.

Labradors grow into fairly big dogs weighing 60–75 lb or more and therefore, need quite an amount of food, but they are very good 'doers' and thrive on simple food, not requiring pampering or tempting with titbits. Indeed, the main difficulty is keeping them slim, because they are inherently greedy and will eat all that's set before them (and the cat's food too, if they get half a chance). The full details of their food will be given in the chapter on management, but compared with other breeds, some smaller dogs eat quite as much as a Labrador, and their equals in size often need and eat a good deal more food. So they can be rated as economical feeders compared with other dogs of their size, provided the 'feeder' is sensible and keeps a strict eye on their waistline, and is impervious to blackmailing glances and hints at mealtimes.

Contrary to popular belief, Labradors are not a breed that require an enormous amount of exercise. People seem to think that they require ten miles or at least four miles a day. This is actually not true. They need to be let out as frequently as any other breed to stretch their legs, limber up and spend their pennies. Apart from this, a short morning walk and a good walk in the evening, or vice versa, will keep the dog fit and well, and if he gets some free galloping and a small amount of walking on hard roads during these walks, he will be fit enough to do a full day's shooting without distress, whenever it is required of him.

For some reason Labradors, which originally came from cold, bleak Newfoundland, seem to do just as well in hot weather as in cold and, indeed, thrive in any climate. It was interesting to me to go to Africa to judge Labradors both at Field Trials and in a blazing sunny show ring, and then to return home to icy winds and snow having found the 'hot dogs' just as fit and well and enjoying their lives as much as my frozen snow-covered northern icicles. So they seem to do well in any climate, provided they are treated correctly, well looked after, and given a little consideration and plenty of access to water.

Compared with these many positive virtues their snags are remarkably few, but it is necessary to consider them before you finally decide on a Labrador, or indeed any dog at all. In fact very few of the snags are found in Labradors alone, most of them being shared by any other breed or variety, even mongrels. For example, in any breed small puppies grow into larger dogs and it is the *final* size of the breed you must consider in conjunction with your own personal circumstances, e.g. whether you have a garden, whether your house is tiny or whether you can spare the cash to have a kennel and run (which I advise if possible for a Labrador, even though it may live in the house). But remember that these considerations apply to any largish breed of dog, which may perhaps be boisterous as a youngster, full of life and bounce. He will not sit all day doing nothing but will need some outdoor exercise, a biggish bed and a considerable amount of good food, more than he can get from household scraps.

Another thing you must consider is that *any* dog, whether Labrador or Great Dane, Pug, Cairn or even mongrel, needs daily attention, wet or fine, hot or snowing, whether you are feeling fit and well, or ill and 'not in the mood'. Every single day of their life, some time and attention, even if only a little, must be given to them. They cannot be put away into the toy-cupboard when you go on holiday and forgotten. Arrangements must be made for them, and their welfare thought of just as you would think of your children if they were to be left for any time at all. If you live alone and go out to work, but want a Labrador as companion, someone should see to him once during the day, unless you have a kennel and run, otherwise a lonely dog will bark and bark until eventually it starts to tear up the cushions and curtains in its desperation. So before you acquire any dog, think of what you will do with it if, say, you are on holiday abroad for a fortnight, or even away from home all day. This problem is no different for a Labrador than for any other dog or pet, but it must be faced. If you can solve it by thinking it out, then certainly keep a Labrador, because they settle easily in a boarding kennel or with friends, soon looking on their holiday quarters as a second home.

Like any other active workmanlike dog, Labradors need discipline. This must be given while they are young, simply for the reason that they grow into biggish dogs. If left to themselves they would become bouncy and unruly, pulling on the lead, getting under your feet and becoming very strong, indeed headstrong. Yet again, this is the same for any dog of any biggish active breed, but here the Labrador's virtues get to work and because they are such good-hearted, kind dogs and eager to please, they very soon respond to training and give up their youthful foolishness and wilfulness, becoming honest, responsible and trustworthy citizens as they reach maturity.

So you must be prepared to be firm with your puppy, insisting on good behaviour and obedience from the first. Otherwise it may grow into an unruly nuisance, like any other undisciplined dog, pulling on the lead, causing accidents, fighting other dogs, and generally making life a misery for you, your neighbours, the local farmers and even the police. So without being savage and harsh, teach and maintain discipline and your Labrador will reward you by developing its inbuilt qualities of being a good house and family dog and the best companion you and your children can have.

If you are prepared to have a medium to biggish dog when adult, to give it a bit of room and a couple of strolls a day, proper care and training, good food and a decent bed, then I can give you no better advice than 'get a Labrador'. If you are the right sort of owner, then the Labrador is the right sort of dog, and you will never regret owning one.

How to Set About Getting a Labrador

Having decided, as I hope you have, to get a Labrador, then before leaping you must look, and look carefully. In other words, do your homework. Read all you can on the breed, talk to people who know about them. Your local pet shop or any local dog-breeder will tell you the name and address of the most reputable Labrador breeder in the district; if they do not know of a local one they will look in their Christmas numbers of the dog papers such as *Dog World,* which supply lists of breeders and will give you the name and address of a breeder in whichever area of Britain you live.

Alternatively you can get the name of the local Canine Secretary; virtually every district is covered by some Canine Club or Association. If you contact the Secretary you will find him very anxious to help you, and he will give you the name of the most reputable Labrador breeder he knows. He will also tell you of any Shows, Working Tests or Field Trials about to take place, to which you could go to contact the Labrador breeders gathered there. Talk, if possible, to an established, experienced breeder whose Kennel is well-known and respected. You will find that the old established breeder is always ready with help and advice, but you will also be asked questions, such as: 'Do you want a dog or a bitch?' 'Black or Yellow or possibly Liver (chocolate)?' 'Do you want a Field Trialler, a shooting dog, a show dog, a bitch to breed from, or a companion?' 'Do you want a big one or medium-to-small?' 'An adult, youngster or small puppy?' If you have done your homework as I suggest, you will be able to give the answer to some of these questions at least, and will be able to consult the breeders and consider their advice on those you can't yet answer.

You in your turn will be armed with questions. 'Will your particular strain of Labrador do the job for which I require it?' 'How much should I pay?' 'Will this strain be good with children?' 'Will I be able to show it, breed from it, train it to decent shooting standard, or even run it in Trials?' Different strains are bred for different jobs, therefore you must already know for what purpose you require a Labrador so that you are sure of getting the right strain. You will also ask questions about food and how much to give, exercise, accommodation, kennels and bedding, and what to do when you get the dog home. If in any doubt about either the breeder's questions or your own, don't be in too much of a hurry. Do as much of your thinking as possible *before* you buy, so that you will be fully prepared to get the dog settled properly and happily on its first night with you in its new home.

When you eventually decide exactly what you want – dog or bitch, colour, specific purpose if any, eventual size age and the approximate price – go to your chosen breeder, lay out the facts and ask him either to show you suitable stock to choose from or to tell you where such a dog is likely to be found.

The vast majority of people who buy Labradors each year are ordinary families wanting a nice, friendly house-companion and pet to share their life and be the family dog. For this purpose I suggest you go to a reputable show breeder. They often have puppies suitable as pets for sale, because show dogs have to have certain specific anatomical and Breed points, and unless they have the basic show qualities are no good for show. In spite of failing in some small show-points, in every other way the puppies you will be shown are the equal of their better-looking brothers, the fault being something like a curly tail or perhaps big ears or spread feet. If you really only want a pet then I advise one of these. They are usually most satisfactory buys as pets and companions, are very good-tempered and have all the attributes of a good family dog.

However if you do get one of these, don't think you are buying a show dog. As I say, the necessary points for show are specific, and if you want to do a bit of showing or to breed eventually from your bitch puppy to produce a show winner for yourself, then go to the same kennel, but pay rather more and get a promising show puppy. It's worth the money and will pay in the long run if the puppy fulfils its promise.

If you want a shooting dog then you *must* go to a good working strain. You can waste a lot of time and money trying to train a puppy that has little or no work bred in it. Many people will tell you that all Labradors will work. I wish they did, but unfortunately this is not true, unless perhaps you add the words 'after a fashion'. A good shooting dog needs just as many specific points as does a show dog – for example, tender mouth, no tendency to whine, speed, good nose, persistence, game-sense, natural retrieving and marking ability, freedom from gun-shyness and a host of other qualities that cannot be tested in the show ring. The virtues of a good gun dog are hereditary and if you want to own or 'make' one, then the parents and ancestors *must* have the qualities themselves. Many of the best show kennels work

A group of the author's dual-purpose dogs. Left to right: (sitting) Ch. Mansergh Moleskin, Ch. M. Antonia, (behind) Ch. Groucho of Mansergh, Ch. Damson of Mansergh, (lying down) American Ch. Mansergh Moose, Black Spice of Mansergh, Doncebelle of Mansergh.

their dogs regularly and most successfully as shooting and Trial dogs, so these are the kennels to visit to get a shooting dog. If it is also good-looking enough for show, then you have the best of both worlds and will enjoy your dog all the more. If, however, you are wanting a high-powered Field Trialler, then you *must* go to a kennel that runs its dogs *successfully* in Trials. Again, Trial dogs need specific qualities, and the ordinary Labrador, as a rule, does not have all these qualities. Like the ordinary shooting dog, the Trialler must have speed, persistence, game-sense, marking ability, tender mouth, silent work, freedom from gun-shyness and all the other qualities that go to make a good gun dog, but they must also have an exceptional ability to understand advanced hand and whistle signals and possess the cool steadiness of character to 'take' these signals, often in most tempting circumstances. So for a Trialler, go to a true working and Trial kennel, and if you can find or breed a good-looker with the essential Trial qualities of steady temperament and deep intelligence then you are lucky indeed.

To sum up, make up your mind exactly what you are going to want from your Labrador, find out which kennel breeds what by talking to the breeders, and buy accordingly.

COLOUR
There is one easy answer to the question 'What colour shall I buy?' and that is, 'Buy the colour you yourself like.' If you are fixed on the idea

of a Yellow, then don't be persuaded to buy a Black or a Liver by anyone, and also don't buy the 'wrong' colour just because the colour you really want is not available.

Most pet purchasers of family dogs seem to go for Yellows which make very good house dogs and companions. They do have an odd snag, which is that they seem to cast their coats constantly, a little at a time. On the other hand, Blacks cast their coats in one fell swoop, filling your dustbin with what looks like a sheep's fleece. I tell you this so that you can make a decision for yourself. As one of our more popular breeders put it, 'It all depends whether you prefer yellow hairs in the blackcurrant jam, or black hairs in the butter.' There is a third possibility of course, and that is 'Liver hairs on the chocolate biscuits.' Liver is the correct word for what is now often called Chocolate.

From the show point of view, if you want your dog to show up well in the ring, then a Yellow often looks much better than a Black. They seem to have more substance, to stand out from most backgrounds better and in a dark hall, or in the dusk of a late show, can be seen, when a Black is disappearing into the shadows. For work, however, I myself plump for a Black. They are usually rather speedier and often much more persistent. I may be accused of bias, seeing that my two nicknames in Labradors are Black-Hearted Mary or The Black Queen (or so I'm told). But I will also point out that I am not alone in this choice and that at nearly every shoot with six or eight guns, keepers, pickers-up etc., the Blacks will far outnumber the Yellows. Also, there will be a vast preponderance of Blacks running and applying to run in Field Trials, when only the best will do for the professional trainers and handlers. These people are practical and experienced and have good reasons for anything they do. If a good Yellow crops up, then they will run it and make it a F.T. Champion without prejudice. But there must be ten black F.T. Champions to every yellow one and the proof of the pudding is in the eating. So whilst I recommend Yellow as the best colour for show, I suggest Black for working purposes and Trials, as most of the true working strains are black.

Liver seems to throw very good dual-purpose dogs for work as well as for show, but of course as there are so few of them there have only been three Champions as yet and no F.T. Champions at all that I know of in this country.

SEX

As with colour, the choice of sex of your new dog is yours alone and probably needs more thought than any other bit of homework so far. You may know immediately which suits your purpose best. For instance, if you are a keen shooting man or a Field Trial enthusiast you will probably know already that you want a dog (male) so that no shooting days or Trials are missed through the bitch being in season. Or if you are starting a breeding kennel then you will (or should) want a bitch, a dog being no use to you to found your kennel, although you will undoubtedly want to keep a dog later on.

So for specific jobs you will know what you want, but it is not so easy for those who just want a nice house pet and companion.

The point that matters most in this case is whether you can manage a bitch 'in season' (the term we use for a bitch that is sexually interesting to the dog, 'on heat' being an alternative term). Many pet-owners dread this moment, or to be more precise these three weeks, which occurs roughly every six or seven months, usually in spring and autumn.

Certainly in most localities there is a problem here. For three weeks you will have to keep your bitch very safe and, indeed, in purdah. She will be keen to escape, behave in a rather flighty and silly manner, and worse still, the dogs of the district will be queueing up to take advantage of any forgetfulness or lack of care on your part. A bitch in this mood is difficult to keep safe, trying every possibility of getting away with a suitor, and the dogs will be equally enterprising at finding the least chink to get to her. So for three weeks every six months, you do have a difficult problem. Indeed, to my mind if you are keeping a bitch you *must* have somewhere absolutely safe where you can shut her up for this period; alternatively many people send their bitches to a boarding kennel when 'on heat', which is usually very satisfactory.

But do not think that this problem only occurs with bitches, because I will remind you that while a bitch is 'in season' only twice a year, your dog might just as well be 'in season' all the year round; he will be watching every lamp-post in the neighbourhood, every tuft of grass and every street corner to get a clue as to which bitch in the neighbourhood is 'interesting', and he will be fretting to get there all the time and escaping if he can. So the swings and the roundabouts work out about even; both dog and bitch are nuisances in the spring and autumn, and you will need a safe place for either at certain times of the year. So my advice on the subject of 'which sex?' is to buy a dog if you are wanting a shooting or Trial dog, but otherwise to buy a bitch. My reasons are that while a dog is after bitches all the time, a bitch is only 'in season' twice a year and is so much easier to handle the rest of the time, having her mind constantly on you, the dog's mind is only half on you if there is a bitch on heat anywhere near. Also, a bitch always seems to me to be slightly kinder, softer-natured, more affectionate and easier to deal with.

So to sum up; a dog for work, a bitch as a pet or to found a kennel.

SIZE
Size is purely a matter of taste, depending on the size of your house,

your garden or your car. It is impossible to give specific advice on the matter of size for work, because some people like a large dog who can fly over seven-barred gates and barbed wire without any trouble at all, while other shooting men know they will be going up to the butts, or from drive to drive in a crowded Land Rover or estate wagon with dogs galore, beaters, keepers, guns and all their clobber. These owners usually like a smaller dog that can tuck away easily into a small space. So my advice here is, make up your own mind about this and then tell the breeder what size you prefer in the grown dog and ask whether the puppy for sale will be big or small in maturity. Experienced breeders know the usual size of their stock, which bitches throw big puppies, how big the sire is, and what he throws. They can help you get what you want, provided of course that you know what you want yourself and have done your homework properly.

COST

Nowadays it is impossible to say exactly what a puppy will cost, with the price of food, petrol and every kennel expense rising almost weekly.

The only real clue I can give you is that the cost of a puppy is usually about double or slightly more than double the stud fee of the sire. Also *bitches* are usually more expensive than dogs, contrary to popular belief. Many years ago dogs cost £5 or £6 more than bitches, but times have changed, and now you can expect to pay quite a lot more for a bitch. I am speaking of the average puppy in the litter. If you want the first or second pick, I must warn you that you are unlikely to get the first pick of bitches and may be lucky to get the second. For first or second pick of a good litter you may have to pay a pretty high price, possibly four times the stud fee, but for reasons which I will explain later in this chapter I can assure you that usually this extra cost is money well-spent.

So for an average, decent puppy, you will probably be asked about double the stud fee for the sire, but for a good bitch puppy (the best buy you can make), be prepared to pay as much as you can for the best you can get.

Beware if you see puppies advertised for sale in your local paper at very low prices. You pay for what you get and get what you pay for, and these puppies for which you pay only a few pounds are in the end not worth even a few pence, and are almost invariably a bad buy.

Above all, beware of buying from the huge all-breeds dealers' kennels. In such large establishments, containing a hundred dogs or so, there is *always* infection of some sort, mange or other skin trouble, tummy troubles of every kind, or possibly even distemper. You may be lucky enough to get a nice puppy from one of these dealers, but one can seldom be sure that the pedigree supplied applies to the dog purchased, and you are likely to get at least one of the above troubles with your new puppy as well. Large numbers of dogs collected from anywhere and everywhere, and dozens of litters bred weekly, always carry trouble. Buy from a genuine breeder instead.

I particularly warn potential buyers to avoid taking a dog from a rescue or lost-dogs' home. Nine times out of ten, a rescued dog is there for a bad reason, having been picked up straying, or perhaps having become too unruly and boisterous for his owners. Worse still, he may have some hidden vice like biting children, chasing and worrying sheep, or simply tearing up the house and home.

Although occasionally a Labrador of good temperament may find its way into one of these homes by genuine misadventure, such as the owner dying or going to hospital, it is very much more likely to be there because of a definite fault. Why buy trouble? So although it may gladden your heart to think you have 'saved' a Labrador and given it a good home, remember that, as in dogs from dealers' kennels, there is very often a fault in a 'lost' dog which will crop up sooner or later and cause you bother, or even serious trouble. A stray will eventually stray again, a boisterous dog will already have learned bad habits, the biter will bite again and the sheep-chaser will chase again. If this last should pick up a companion and start to kill sheep, it may land you with a fearful bill, and itself a death sentence.

A kennel owner that dealt with these stray dogs recently gave me the principal reasons for Labradors coming in to them. She said that the large majority of these were very big, young dogs, for some reason nearly always yellow (I am quoting, not writing from bias; the possible reason is that yellows are often bigger than blacks at the boisterous stage, and therefore cause perhaps more trouble while young).

The reasons most often given for abandoning dogs to the rescue schemes were these: 'He won't come when called, he jumps up all the time and pulls me all over the place.' 'He steals *everything*.' 'He barks all day while we are at work and the neighbours are complaining.' 'The moment we let him out he goes off and we don't see him again all day. We often have to go to the police station and collect him.' 'The farmer saw him chasing sheep; he had a lamb in his mouth.' 'We can't keep him out of water and he brings in mud and Mother is so houseproud.' And lastly, 'He sheds hair all over everything.'

It is comparatively easy to deal with all these things if you have the dog from the beginning and if you are firm with him, but once he has started bad habits it is terribly difficult to get him to change his ways.

If you buy from an experienced breeder's kennel these bad habits will not yet have developed and then it is up to you to see they don't start. Never buy a dog which has to be cured of something bad before you start.

AGE

The final decision you must make before your homework is completed is this: at what age do you buy your Labrador?

Many people, when buying a pet, find it best to book a puppy as soon as (or even before) it is born. This is a good thing to do in many ways and is the most usual. You can go with the children to see the puppies when they are a week or two old and can choose the one you like at about six weeks. You can collect it at eight to eight and a half weeks, when it is quite ready to leave its mother. You can then settle it nicely in your home and steer it the way you want it to live, from the very beginning of its separate existence as an individual. In other words you can 'bring it up in your own way'. This is initially the cheapest way of buying a puppy, as it is practically at cost price, having only been weaned from its mother's milk three or four weeks, and not having been inoculated. At this age puppies are very easy to settle, although they will be lonely for the first day or two (and especially at night) because they have never been alone before. But they soon get the hang of things and are settled right into the routine for life. An old hearth-brush in their bed gives them both a toy and something bristly to snuggle up to.

I recommend this age for the average buyer and, indeed, for the majority of buyers who just want a house and family pet, as you do not have to pay out too much money all at once.

For more serious beginners, who are laying the foundation of a breeding or show kennel, it is better to buy at a later date, when the breeder has 'run on' two or three of the very best puppies from the litter for her own selection (as I always do myself). Very often these two or three are extremely high-class puppies, and after the breeder has eventually decided on the very best for his or her own purposes, the other one or two, who will still be especially good puppies, may be for sale. These are the ones I recommend for the potentially serious beginner, to found a kennel. They will cost a lot more than the eight-week-old puppy, being themselves about five to seven months, but they will still be with the breeder because they are extra good puppies worth running on to this age, and therefore you are buying a very good proposition indeed. The breeder's own final selection will certainly be the best of the puppies retained, but the second one will be good too. So I recommend the second of those that have been run on deliberately by the breeder as a *very* good proposition and buy, even if you do have to pay more. I have sold many excellent 'second selections' which have done really well for their buyers, making a grand foundation for their kennels.

These older puppies may be very expensive compared with the eight-week ones, but they have three great benefits for their buyer:

the buyer can see for certain (1) that the teeth etc., have come right; (2) that the puppy is shapely and has good feet, head, tail, etc; (3) that it is well-grown, having been reared by an experienced breeder. Also, the puppy will be over teething troubles, will have been inoculated, and has lived to the age of four to seven months without having a stunting set-back, is approximately the right size for its age, and above all is not nervous, (a highly hereditary fault). So you pay more, but are not buying a 'pig in a poke' as you undoubtedly are when buying from the nest, in which case you (and not the breeder) run the risks of the puppy dying, suddenly stopping growing, teething wrong, or having a set-back after its injection. So for a potential show exhibitor and breeder, the older puppy is cheapest in the long run.

Opinions differ as to what age to buy for work. The ideal is to breed your own worker, but you have to make a start somewhere, and shooting men seldom want to be bothered with breeding puppies, many of them owning dogs, not bitches, anyway.

For training, some people like to know absolutely everything that has happened to a puppy from the moment it left the nest and became an individual at eight weeks. Others like the puppy to be actually ready for training, so that it can go straight from the breeder to the trainer and be ready to do a bit of light work towards the end of the next shooting season. This again is a good way for the ordinary one-dog shooting man, because the trainer gets 'virgin soil' on which to work; the puppy has been in the hands of the breeder up to that time, and has not learnt bad 'pet' tricks such as pulling toys away from the children, or tearing up cushions and enjoying romping about with the flying feathers, both bad habits for potential gun dogs.

As I breed my own working dogs and potential gun dogs, and always have done since my first buy, it is hard for me actually to advise on an age, not knowing whether you intend to train your shooting dog yourself. But I lay out the possibilities for your careful consideration as to whether you want a young 'unprinted' puppy, an older 'ready to train' puppy of, say seven months or, the last possibility, to open your purse, lay down several hundred pounds and buy a ready-made, ready-trained shooting dog, which is a very successful method for the wealthy buyer. But I venture to guess that by no means all readers, nor for that matter I, come into that last category, much though we should like it.

Picking Your Puppy

If you have a choice of puppies of the right colour and sex, there are certain specific things to look for to help you in your choice.

First a warning. For some reason, perhaps because they are little, rather helpless and may be knocked about by their big brothers, many people fall for the runt, the smallest, weakest, and often the bravest and cockiest puppy, in the litter. They appeal immensely to the best side of human nature, and many people actually make a point of choosing them. But before you do so, remember that they may have wonderful characters and plenty of pluck – indeed they would not have survived unless they had these qualities – but they are not a very good proposition because of their runtiness. The smallness and weakness comes from natural causes, and while they are very sweet and appealing they are not good propositions. It is wiser to choose one of the good strong ones who have *not* had to struggle to keep up or get any food at all, and have not probably been slightly short of food for the first four weeks while trying to get to the 'milk-bar' against stronger competition.

Look for a good, strongly built, healthy-looking puppy, with no trace of nerves, lively and friendly. The head and muzzle should be broad, with a good length of neck, well laid-back shoulders, true elbows and straight, sound bone in the limbs. Look for a short, sturdy body with round ribs, a feeling of tightness and not slackness or limpness when the puppy is picked up, a nice solid firm back and a short thick tail. Watch the puppy when it is eating, drinking, or spending a penny, to see that the tail does not curl up over the back. These are the moments when a high-carried curly tail shows. The eyes should be clean and bright and must not be yellow-coloured or unduly light. The ears should be smallish and neat and, contrary to popular fancy, the feet should *not* be huge and floppy, but instead round and compact and not too obviously over-large.

Huge spreading feet are an ugly fault in an adult Labrador, as are big, heavy, hanging ears. The coat should be dense and clean, without coatless patches and the whole puppy well-grown, short-bodied and sturdy-looking; alert, playful and active. Beware of the puppy that sits about by itself. It may be blind or have hip dysplasia (see the chapter on ailments). Above all, it is character and temperament that count, so make sure the puppy is happy-natured and not sulky and surly, and that it shows no signs of temper or nerves whatsoever, and will play lightly, actively and freely with the other puppies, and your children too.

2 Puppy Management

Having decided on your puppy, big or small, the first thing you must do before fetching it from the breeder is to make provision for its first night with you, in the way of food, a warm bed, and where the bed is going to stand.

It is as well when you book the puppy to find out from the breeder what food it will have been weaned on to and is therefore used to. Get in a smallish supply, because a puppy does not stay long on the same food, and until you have full instructions from the breeder as to the first three or four months, it is wise just to get enough for the first few days until you see what food and how much you need. The puppy will need a warm bed in a draught-proof place, neither too hot nor at all chilly. The puppy will need to be snug the first night, as up to then it has always snuggled up to its brothers and sisters.

I like a high-sided box for the very first evening, so that the puppy is not tempted to climb out of it and sleep on a cold floor, perhaps pressed against the crack under the door, where it may get thoroughly chilled, which is lethal to a small puppy. So I suggest a high-sided box with a bit of blanket laid over a newspaper, or a good bed of straw. After the first night, the puppy needs to be able to get out and (very important) to get back in if it falls out by mistake.

There are two important things about the position of the bed. It must not stand on a stone or cement floor, from which the chill strikes up, but on something like linoleum or an old bit of carpet, the bed slightly raised if possible. Also, on no account put the bed at the foot of the Aga, Rayburn or other solid-fuel cooker or boiler, unless the bed is raised. The solid fuel gives off heavy fumes which stay in a layer on the floor and if your bed is low, the puppy may sleep in a layer of fumes and suffer the consequences. I have known this happen all too often, so if possible *never* let your dogs or cats sleep at the foot of the cooker or hot-water boiler. The fumes can *kill*.

Having made all possible preparations, take some newspaper for the car, because you will probably have a very sick puppy on the way home. If you can, take someone with you to have the puppy on their knee so that it does not wander all over the car. If this is not possible, then take your deep box in which it is going to spend the first night. A strong, deep cardboard box does very well. The stiff carton you get your groceries in is very good, being warm and strong enough to last a

Sh. Ch. Crawcrook
Princess.

few days, and an entrance can be cut on the second day when the
puppy has spent the first night safely in bed. Don't forget your cheque
book or cash for the purchase (plus the cost of the injection if the
puppy has been inoculated). Make absolutely sure that the puppy has
been wormed, and had its toe-nails cut. If they haven't been cut, ask the
breeder to do this at once. It only takes a few seconds and is simple for
any experienced person but is a bit nerve-racking for someone who has
never cut a dog's toe-nails before.

Also, make sure the puppy is free of vermin, because puppies very
often pick up undesirable 'guests' from the straw bedding. If in doubt,
the breeder will dust it over for you, just to make sure.

Don't forget to ask the breeder about the diet for the next few weeks,
also how and when to get the puppy inoculated against hardpad, distemper and any form of jaundice.

The breeder will give you advice as to this but you must also check
with your vet when you get the puppy well settled, so that you get it
done when he advises. Whatever you do, have it done, because there is
nothing so heart-breaking as getting fond of your first puppy and then
have it terribly ill and dying because you have not taken this simple
precaution.

Remember to ask the breeder whether the puppy has been vaccinated, and consult your vet as soon as possible about when to get it
done, and what injection to have.

Ch. Savrona Gem of Gems of Kerlstone.

Then, having asked all the important questions, pay your money and collect the puppy's papers. These will consist of a pedigree signed by the breeder, the Kennel Club Registration Certificate, if the breeder has registered it, and a signed Kennel Club Transfer Form, so that you can put it officially into your name in their registers. If, however, the breeder has *not* registered the puppy, make sure you get a Form for Registration of the puppy from the breeder, duly signed by him and fully in order with all the necessary numbers etc., filled in so that you can register it yourself. Make sure you have these papers all in order. If the puppy has been inoculated, get the vaccination certificate (although usually the puppy is too young at this stage for this). However, it is always as well to ask about the vaccination, as very young puppies may be immunised temporarily by a measles injection, and this affects the subsequent 'real' inoculation.

Then collect your puppy and get it home, keeping it warm on the journey.

House-training

House-training should start from the very beginning. Immediately *after every* meal or snack, the puppy should be set down, outside, or on a newspaper if you have to, always in the same place so that it learns to use the same spot every time. Once it has learned to use the newspaper it can be moved nearer to the door each day, until the puppy learns to go out for the necessary few minutes. There is no difficulty in house-training a Labrador if it is put out and watched for a minute or two after every meal. That is the way nature works, and the dog will very soon learn to wait till put out and then to use exactly the same spot in the garden, where you have started it from the beginning. It will soon become a creature of habit.

There is more difficulty about the wet 'penny' than the solid 'two-pence', which is easy to teach, but anticipation by you yourself is the cure for the puppy wetting indoors. Get that puppy out just *before* it is thinking of wetting. You know better than it how long it is since it last went out. Remember that little puppies' bladders are very small, so it needs putting out often at first, until the bladder becomes larger and stronger. The great blessing is that, believe it or not, the Labrador likes to be clean and to have one place to relieve itself, and once it has learned this spot it will try and always use it. So if your puppy considers that the middle of the sitting-room floor is its place, that is your fault for not getting it into the habit of always going under the holly bush or in the shrubbery or wherever you prefer to the house.

You must carefully consider his future accommodation. Please don't let your poor puppy have to sleep just where he happens to find himself in your house. If he lives indoors, get him a proper dog's bed, so that he can go to bed as well as you. I am always horrified when staying with friends who have 'good homes' for their dogs (or so they think) to find the dog has to sleep bare on the landing or just lying on the floor in the hall. He likes a comfortable bed, just as you do, and actually needs it. So see he has his own bed, raised off the floor, inside a room if possible, not in a draughty hall or passage. If he has such a bed, let sleeping dogs lie during the day. They need a tremendous amount of sleep and get very highly strung and full of tension if they do not get regular periods of sleep. Let him rest when he wants to and do not allow the children to keep waking him up just for the fun of it. He will play a lot with the children, but while he is young let him have those long periods of rest he so badly needs. At first he may sleep 18 hours or more out of the 24.

It does not matter what the bed is made of, so long as it is big enough for him to stretch out, is really warm, and if possible deep so that he can snuggle his back against the back of the bed. A puppy's kidneys are very vulnerable to draught, and should be given protection if possible. There are plenty of such beds on the market ready for when he leaves his cardboard carton.

When young, a silly little puppy will try and lie on the floor instead of his bed; do not let him do this. He *must* get into the habit of sleeping in his bed. This useful habit will pay you in the long run, especially if he prefers his bed to the best place on the hearth-rug, which your visitors like too.

Feeding

Food is a very important thing to the growing puppy, much more so than to the biggest adult dog. Labradors are good trenchermen by nature and will eat everything (and unfortunately anything, even down to empty glass jam jars if there is a trace of flavour in them). A young puppy has been used to taking a suck off his mother whenever he feels like it, even if half asleep. He has therefore been used to umpteen tiny snacks whenever he felt like one. But now things are different, and his breeder will have already got him on to regular feeds.

My regime is this. At 8 weeks old my puppies are on four meals a day (although many people prefer five). For breakfast mine have puppy-meal (Number One size) soaked in hot water or a little hot milk. To this is added each day a sprinkling of a calcium–vitamin D product and also some coddled egg and a tablespoonful of meat, scraps, or a bit of mince. They wolf this easily digested meal, digestibility being essential when puppies need nutrients quickly after a long night without food. The puppies are then put out for playtime and to 'do the necessary', usually in a play-pen I have constructed for their early days. Any corner that has not got precious plants in it will do, because all you need is a wire pen that you can bend over to pick up and remove either a dish or a puppy. It is a very useful thing to have such a play-pen, which can be bought at a pet shop, or made in a corner of a yard or garden. This saves you a lot of hanging about while a puppy is playing, and provided there is a suitable floor to it, of grass, gravel or wood, then a puppy can spend quite a bit of time in it, always remembering three rules: (1) puppies must have long stretches of sleep after a very few minutes' play; (2) they must be warm and must not lie on cold damp surfaces; (3) they need shade and water. A puppy should, therefore, have a raised wooden board to lie on while he sleeps, if he is to be left out of doors for more than ten minutes, and he must have shade and water if the sun is hot. A Labrador puppy, however young, has a dense coat and a normal temperature of 38.9° C (102° F), so he boils up very easily and can get thoroughly overheated, which may result in a bad chill afterwards. So have a play-pen if you possibly can, but remember he is only a small baby as yet and must be treated as such; use your common sense about him just as you would with a human baby.

His second meal is at noon, when he gets enough raw butcher's mince (even though it is very expensive) to make a nice 'ball' in his tummy. He does not want to be either blown out with meat, nor starved, so look at his tummy and consider the amount for yourself. I give a little milk, cold but not chilled, with the meat. In the evening, about 6 o'clock, he has a larger repeat of his breakfast, but soaked with broth, not milk. This is his main meal, and he can have meat, fish, scraps, broth, cooked or raw meat on it. The consistency of the soaked meal should be crumbly, not soggy. Don't give him more egg at night, because one coddled egg on his breakfast is quite enough for one day. I give him a good supper at this time, so that he starts digesting it when he goes to bed and it lasts most of the night, but at 8 to 11 weeks I do top him up the very last thing at night when I go to bed myself, with Farex made with warm milk, i.e. an easily digestible cereal feed just to keep him happy and warm during the long night.

So the key to a very young puppy's early welfare is: at least four meals a day, warmth in bed, lots of sleep and four regular playtimes after his meals for about ten minutes each, or if he feels lively he may play more often according to his nature. He will sleep when he needs it, provided he is not continually disturbed. His food is made up of the following: biscuit meal soaked with gravy, broth or milk; raw mince; cooked meat; coddled egg; fish; chicken or rabbit; small quantities of chopped vegetables; household scraps (but not instead of meat, rather in addition to it); cheese; brown bread for a change from biscuits occasionally; and a preparation such as Farex. In additives I always give Calcium and Vitamin D on the morning meal, a drop or two (and I mean a drop, not a teaspoon) of cod-liver oil about three times a week, except in high summer, and a vitamin B yeast preparation called Vetzyme if I think he needs building up a bit. The instructions are on the tin. I usually give about five Vetzymes at a time to a young puppy. They are extremely cheap to buy so you can hand them out freely and the puppies soon learn to take them from your hand, because dogs seem to find them delicious. There must *always* be fresh water available for any dog, all his life from 5 weeks onwards.

Besides food, bed, warmth, and play, you must see to two or three things. First, the puppy may have a tummy upset soon after you have him, either from chill, in spite of all your efforts, or more likely from the change of air, water or food, however careful you are. This tummy upset is difficult to deal with, and many people take their puppies anxiously to the vet. This is always a good thing to do if in any doubt, as the vets like to get their patients early before any possible disease gets a strong hold, but remember a vet is a very busy man, so don't worry him too much unnecessarily. For any tummy upset that a puppy has because he has come into my kennel, I do the following, so long as I am sure it is just a tummy upset and the puppy is otherwise perfectly well and lively. I cut out all raw milk for a couple of days, soaking the meal with plain water and giving extra small, rather stiff meals. I give a little raw meat, but no eggs or cooked meat, especially no liver, and I also give the puppy some very stiff rice pudding, made with a mixture of milk and water and a bit of sugar or glucose in it. As he recovers, I mix these rice puddings with rabbit, chicken or meat broth instead of water, so that I am hardening his diet, instead of softening it by giving more milk or slops. Raw cow's milk is a laxative to a puppy, as is sloppy food, but stiff rice pudding lines the stomach and enables it to have a rest. This treatment with stiffer food usually works at once, but if the tummy upset persists or the puppy looks ill and off its food, then I go to the vet at once. This tummy hazard is usually very soon over, after a day or at the most a couple of days.

General Care

TOE-NAILS

I have mentioned cutting the toe-nails; this must be done at least twice during the first few weeks. If done then, it seems to last for life and the toe-nails give little or no trouble. It is so easily done; only your own nerves cause any difficulty. For some reason people *hate* doing it, but if the breeder has not done it, then you must. Wear your old clothes, then a small pair of sharp scissors and a chair is all you need. You only have to take the little sharp tip off. The toe-nail will look like a rose-thorn with a needle-sharp curved tip, which is rather transparent, thickening to a solid base, just like the body of the thorn. Hold the pup on your knee in your *left hand*, head facing towards your right hand, which holds the scissors. Don't be nervous; nothing can go wrong so long as you keep the puppy's tongue and eyes from your scissors. Put the first two fingers and thumb of your left hand, which is over pup's neck, so that they grip the right foot and hold it away from the body. You will see the long, sharp curved tip. Just snip that off, keeping well clear of any thickening of the nail. It will be quite painless, but if you do make a mistake and the pup gives a squeak and a tiny drop of blood comes, don't panic, just go straight on with the others. It does no harm at all, stops hurting immediately and they lose no blood. But actually this unnerving thing will not happen so long as you just snip off the needle-sharp tip. The idea is not to cut the nails right down, but merely to blunt the tip, whereupon the puppy walks on the next bit down, which wears easily on the ground and will then shorten itself while the 'quick' retreats further up the nail. This is the reason why it usually need be done only twice in a Labrador's lifetime. The second cutting again blunts the needle-tip, and then natural wear takes place keeping the nail short for life, provided the dog is getting outdoor exercise, as all Labradors must. It is preferable for you to do this yourself, because you must avoid one thing at all costs, and that is getting the puppy frightened of the vet and his surgery. Dogs that have not had this early treatment or who do not get proper exercise and have to go to the vet's to have their nails cut as adults, can go berserk with fear as they approach the surgery. This can be completely avoided if you quietly cut the puppy's nails yourself between four and ten weeks. While you are doing this don't forget the dew-claws, those little nails on the inside of the dog's forelegs. They may have been removed at birth by the breeder, but most Labrador breeders leave them on, because the dog may need them for carrying pheasants over walls, fences, rocks, and up and particularly down steep banks. They use them as hooks to keep their grip in these cases. So cut the tips of the dew-claws as you do each forefoot (it is very unlikely that there will be any dew-claws on the back feet, as the Labrador breed seems virtually free of hind dew-claws). Just take the sharp needle-tip off, as you do with the rest of the nails.

WORMING

The second essential that you must see to is worming. This will, or ought to have been done at least once by the breeder, but worming only clears the worms that are there already hatched, so a second dose is always needed to clear the latest crop. *Don't blame the breeder* if the puppy has worms. All puppies start life with worms, so the pup *must* be done at least twice, but preferably three times, before 6 months. After that you use your common sense as to whether you need give occasional further doses. It does no harm, and is regular practice in all good breeding kennels, when all adult dogs are dosed at least twice a year. Dogs can and do get infected at any time, so it is no disgrace to you if you find your puppy or adult dog suddenly has worms. He has caught them by ingesting the eggs off the grass he chews for medicinal purposes, or off sheep or rabbits, or perhaps even from his food. Don't curse the breeder or weep with horror and disgrace; just give the dog a pill that you get from the chemist or vet. Puppies always have round-worms until dosed; adult dogs have tape-worms very occasionally, especially if they have been on sheep or rabbit ground. The pills for round- and tape-worms are different, so if under 6 months ask for round-worm tablets, but over 6 months ask for tape-worm tablets.

There are four things which can be fed to help the puppy keep clear of worms. They are raw meat without any additive, boiled apple peel (I think that the obvious reason for the adage that 'an apple a day keeps the doctor away' was because in the old days worms in children and indeed adults must have been a major cause of ill health and weakness before we found cures for worms), raw egg, and the water in which onions or onion peel have been boiled. Many people swear by raw garlic, which certainly does the trick, but is difficult to use without that revolting smell.

INOCULATION

I have now given you three of the 'musts' for growing puppies, which it is your responsibility to see done; tummy upset cleared up, nails cut, worm-dose given. I come to the last, inoculation against the three major diseases, distemper, hepatitis and jaundice. This inoculation, which is of vital importance, must be done at exactly the correct time and not put on one side 'until you have time'. I am not going to say categorically what brand of vaccine you must use, because your vet will know what he likes for dogs and will know exactly when he wants you to bring the puppy, whether to give a second injection and, if so, how long after the first (this double injection is the most common nowadays). If you hear there is distemper in your neighbourhood (beware of that roaming dog) or if one of your own dogs or a neighbour's develops distemper symptoms, then your young puppy is at risk. There is a measles injection which also acts for puppies against distemper, and this can be given for immediate protection although a proper vaccine must be given later on in addition. This measles vaccine can be given to very young puppies, even in the nest, so in emergency, it can be resorted to as an immediate temporary protection to the youngest pup. But there must be a genuine emergency, because it has recently been discovered that the puppies of a bitch that herself has been given the measles vaccine as a small puppy are immune to it; therefore in a future emergency, when your pup eventually has *her* puppies, *they* cannot be given it because it is useless to them. Before you rush to get your pup done with 'the measles', just stop and think carefully. Is there really enough danger going the rounds to make this essential? If there is, certainly get it done as temporary protection, but remember, you are mortgaging the lives of her future litters if an emergency arises when they are tiny. My advice is never use the measles vaccine unless you have to, and *never* just because it's available, for your peace of mind. Remember those puppies to come, probably several very valuable litters, who will not be able to take it however bad a future crisis they may have to face. They will be forced to await their proper vaccination at a later age, three to four months, and thus may lose their one opportunity to live through a violent epidemic.

Having got the vaccination over, you need to keep your dogs quiet and not take them out into the streets until the injection has had time to work (about ten days with the full inoculation). It is advisable to ask your vet about a 'booster' a year later. This keeps your dogs' immunity to distemper, hepatitis and leptospirosis at the highest possible level, and will give you a feeling of security should an epidemic of any of these terrible diseases break out in your neighbourhood, as often happens in suburbs or farming communities where the general public may not bother with injections.

Kennels

A difficult problem for the new owner is how to kennel the Labrador. This very much depends on your plans for the future with the breed. If you are just buying a pet for the house, then I advise a good indoor bed and, if you can manage it, a railed or chain-linked corner outside where you can put a big kennel to shut your dog in, when you are going out and leaving it behind. I recommend this method because of the tendency to chew cushions, rugs, and curtains if any Labrador gets bored or restless. Also, the dog is presumably already house-trained or is trying his best to be, and it is not only unfair to make him hold his water for long periods because he knows he will be punished for wetting in the house, but it is also dangerous to the dog, who may very well get kidney disease or other troubles at six years old, just because of having to retain his water too long. So if you can, have a safe outdoor kennel for even your house-pet, to pop him in if you are out for a longish period. A big marrow-bone will take care of boredom.

For such a kennel, a shed or big hut will do, but personally I think it is worth spending the extra money and buying a proper kennel and run for him. There are lots on the market of every shape and size to meet your requirements. For someone who plans to start a kennel of Labradors, however small, I advise not just a railed off corner with a shed, but a proper site with a good kennel and run. I would also

Fig 1
The Author's Own
Kennels
Bedrooms (individual) 6 ft × 4 ft
Runs (individual) 6 ft × 4 ft
Shared Runs (daytime) 8 ft × 8 ft

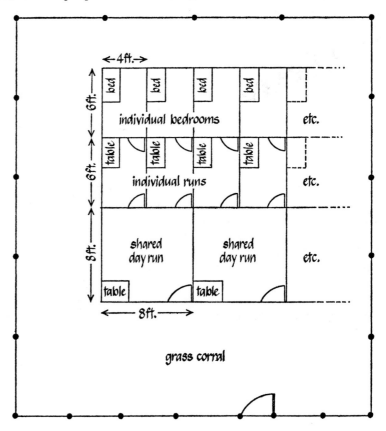

recommend a double kennel, because the first thing you are likely to do in your new venture is to breed from your foundation bitch and keep a daughter. This is how almost every 'strain' starts; it happens very quickly and before you know where you are, probably within a couple of years, you have two Labradors. So while you are having the bother of making a site, a yard and a cement base for your new kennel, you might just as well make a double one. It works out very much cheaper in the end.

In the same way, if your plans are more ambitious and you are thinking of five or six Labradors and going in for it properly, then a range of kennels is a substantial saving of capital, because kennels will almost certainly have risen in price by the next year and astronomically over the five years after you start. So plan *now* for the future; know your purpose with your Labrador, whether house-pet, shooting dog (when a kennel with deep straw is useful after a wet day's shooting even if only to dry the dog off), foundation bitch or small collection of brood bitches or puppies.

I give a plan of a very good kennel range I have now. I said in my first book on the breed (*The Dual-Purpose Labrador*, Pelham Books, 1969) that these were what I should build 'if ever my ship came home' and I had the odd pound or two extra to spend on kennels. Well, it did in a modest sort of way, and I could carry out my longed-for design. I have used it now for some seven years, and it works perfectly. It is based on the simple idea that each dog sleeps alone in his own kennel, in his own bed. He has a bedroom at least 4 ft × 6 ft with a warm bed in the most draught-proof corner in which he can lie flat out if he wants to, and made so that the bedding stays in. Attached to this bedroom is an iron-barred individual run 6 ft × 4 ft, half-roofed over and with a small table or bench on which he can sit and be sheltered by the half roof if it is showery weather. Every dog has this basic-unit individual kennel and run. Every two units open into a bigger iron-barred run, so that the dogs can each sleep in their own bedroom-compartment by night and be shut in their individual run if necessary by day, but normally every dog can share a run with a compatible companion during the day. As the bigger shared double-runs are 8 ft × 8 ft, this means that during the day, when all doors are open, every two dogs share a 20 ft × 8 ft space. Then to be luxurious and to keep the dogs safe from the main road, there is a big compound or corral made of steel mesh right round the entire perimeter, so that on fine days the dogs can all play together or in batches, on grass, outside the kennel-runs altogether. A fenced-in orchard or garden supplies this corral, which you will find keeps the dogs very happy on sunny fine days. I will be mentioning the actual management and use of this big run in a later chapter.

THE DOG BREEDERS ACT 1974

If your new purchase is a bitch (not a dog, as the Act only applies to bitches), you should carefully consider the implications of the Act before actually building kennels. It applies to *everyone* who owns three bitches between the ages of 8 months and 9 years *whether you intend to breed from them or not*. No three bitches are exempt between these ages, unless you can produce a vet's certificate that one or more has been spayed. So, when considering your future establishment, remember you will have to register with your local Council when your new (single) purchase's own bitch puppies are 9 months old and you are keeping them. (You may not expect to, but wait until you see that first litter and those lovely little bitches that are your very first home-bred puppies.) Remember, this increase from one to three bitches can happen within two years of buying your first bitch.

The following are the requirements for each Labrador bitch you keep; they may differ slightly from Council to Council:

1 20 sq. ft of bedroom space, of which at least half must be floor-space (my measurement of 6 ft × 4 ft covers this, being 24 sq. ft).
2 The kennels must be cleaned twice daily, and must have easily cleaned and dried floors.
3 There must be no dark corners; there must be proper ventilation and proper whelping quarters, which should have sufficient light and warmth.
4 There must be proper bedding and the bitch must be able to lie flat on her side in bed. The kennels must be large enough for her to stand up and turn round (my measurements cover this, provided the roof allows for standing-up. I like a 6 ft high ceiling, but the Act does not specify this).
5 There must be facilities for disposing of waste and old bedding etc.
6 The dogs must have wholesome drinking water at all times.
7 They must have regular food and be visited at suitable intervals.
8 Everything must be kept clean and vermin free.
9 If you use meat, there must be refrigeration; and bulk supplies of biscuit or meal must be in rat-proof containers. Flies must be eliminated from the kennels.
10 Heating appliances must be safe and there must be easy access to entrances and exits in case of fire. A fire extinguisher of some sort must be handy and clearly marked.

There are other requirements if you employ staff. Proper registers of your bitches and their 'whelpings' have to be kept.

The above are the main provisions and need to be borne in mind when you plan your kennels, which will be inspected about once a year by a vet or a Council official.

3 Adolescent and Adult Management

The routine of eating, spending a penny or twopence, playing and then sleeping, continues until the puppy is about four months old, although the number of meals is gradually reduced. I start by cutting out the midnight feed at nine or ten weeks. They continue on three meals, breakfast, midday and supper. The midday feed becomes less and less while breakfast and supper get progressively bigger. The great thing is that however many meals you cut out you must *not* reduce the actual food given. The quantity increases, though ending up as only breakfast and dinner; the quality is kept very high with brown bread, biscuit, meat (both raw and cooked), vegetables, broth, milk, eggs, fish, etc., as you can spare them. But remember, though times are hard, you *must* put the best into your puppy at this important age. You can never make up for it later. All the goodness must go in now, during the first five or six months. Some meat is essential for the growing puppy, the quantity increasing as he gets older. Many people try to rear puppies on heart, liver, lights, fish, etc., and call it meat, but it isn't; when I say meat, throughout this book I mean red meat and nothing else, although it can be cooked or raw according to the circumstances. I cannot over-emphasise that at this age the growing puppy must have plenty of top-class food.

Provided he gets this, and is allowed to play as much as he likes and sleep when he wants to, the puppy should go on well. He will have to be wormed again at about five months and, of course, inoculated, and these operations should not be combined, as both are a strain on his constitution. The inoculation should take place when he is three and a half to four months old. Do not have it done unless the puppy is 100-per-cent fit and well; the same applies to worming. Your vet will advise you on this.

With some form of calcium and vitamin D on his breakfast several times a week, a drop of cod-liver oil twice a week in winter, and Vetzyme for a week or so after his injection, your puppy should go ahead like a house on fire both mentally and bodily, making rapid growth during his first six months. I am not against the 'complete food' now on the market and nearly always have a bag of it handy, so that the dogs can have an extra meal in the morning if I think they need it, especially when at the awkward adolescent stage. But I do not approve of it as a life-style, especially from the fertility point of view, and hope that the time will not come when we are forced to use this method because there is no more meat or wholemeal biscuit available. So before you go on to this method to save yourself trouble, just cast a thought to your puppy, one of whose daily highlights is his dinner; make it as tasty and delicious as you can for him. Do not expect him to eat nothing but a 'complete food' (i.e. a dry, dull 'hen-type' mash with no variety or change of taste) for the rest of his life.

As early in the morning as I can, I give the puppies breakfast; you will have the breeder's specific instructions as to the contents. I have given my ideas on breakfast in Chapter 2. Next my puppies have a good run in their grass enclosure. They play until they want to sleep, or lie about and then go to bed for two or three hours. At midday, they have their mince-feed and again the free gallop and play on the grass. Sleep in the afternoon until about 6 p.m., when they have their main, fairly solid meal. Again the run on the grass and then to bed-proper, shut in and piped down for the first part of the night, or the whole night after a week or two.

As the puppy grows towards six months, gradually cut out the midday feed as well as the late-night snack (which I discussed in Chapter 2), until at six months he is on two meals a day: a decent but still easily digested breakfast, with the additives already mentioned, and a jolly good adult supper. These now incorporate the other two snacks, so that you are not giving less food, but more, at two meals only. This goes on until the puppy is eight months old when you may, preferably in summer, try stopping breakfast gradually, giving just a bit of bread or a biscuit instead, or a marrow-bone to chew. The puppy still grows until at least eighteen or twenty months, and must still have top-class nourishment. Keep the additives and the meat going. Of course you need no longer feed mince; that went when the teeth came through to bite and chew meat. The grades of puppy biscuits have got larger, harder to crunch, and the food more adult all the time. The puppy should, however, stay on two meals until eight or ten months according to its build, its hunger, and whether it is a dog or bitch (remember those hungry schoolboys). You must, until eighteen months, be prepared to go back to a big biscuit or door-step of bread for breakfast if the hungry lad looks like going back in condition. At eighteen or twenty months, the appetite will grow much less, and then you can save a bit on food, but not much earlier.

Once the growth has been made and the puppy settles to being a young adult, the rule is one meal a day for life, except in emergencies such as illness, motherhood, etc. Even a hard-working shooting dog sticks to the one-meal rule. But use your common sense and give a biscuit on extra cold mornings, or if the dog is under some stress. These occasions should be fairly rare, and one really good big meal is all that is needed by an ordinary adult leading an ordinary normal life. And *beware*, oh please beware, of those snacks and handouts from the kind neighbour, the butcher, the cook or the children. Watch out too for egg-stealing and dustbin snatching. That gives those tell-tale gross rolls of fat. Do not give the adult Labrador too much meat. I have stressed that you *must* give proper meat and plenty of it in puppyhood, but once adult and mature, then one-quarter meat to three-quarters biscuit meal plus scraps and vegetables is quite enough unless the adult is having or feeding pups, or if a dog has had a succession of bitches at stud to him, or if the shooting season is in full swing and the dog is in very hard daily work. Then extra meat must or may be given.

No hard-and-fast rule can be laid down; use your common sense, and if you feel an adult or youngster needs more meat, give it, but remember that too much meat is as bad as too little, if not worse. In its natural state a dog eats a lot of grass and also the entrails of anything it kills or finds for food, thus getting vegetable food as well as meat. For this reason I always feed vegetables or vegetable-water several times a week. I cook the outside leaves of cabbages or cauliflowers and chop them up, also carrots, onions, apple-peel and apple cores. If it is a bad time for green vegetables, I cook nettles with the meat and feed the dogs the broth on the biscuit. Nettles are exceptionally good for dogs, as they contain a lot of iron, and they help skin trouble, pinkness of the skin, and any itch except mange, which is not caused by overheated blood but by a mite. Boil the nettles well, exactly as you pull them. When cooked, scrape off the green leaves, just like asparagus or spinach, and feed with the meat. The dogs will love the dinner that contains nettles.

Once or twice a week give the dog a huge marrow-bone (raw, never cooked) to chew. He will love it, it keeps him entertained for hours and does his teeth a tremendous amount of good, cleaning them beautifully, and also giving him much-needed calcium. Never give cooked bones of any sort, and *never* give rabbit, game, chicken or fish bones. They are extremely dangerous to a dog. On the other hand don't panic if your dog does find a chicken leg at a picnic site and wolfs it. The odds are very strong that one bone won't hurt him, but if you gave chicken bones regularly the worst just might happen, and a sharp end perforate the bowel. Don't take the risk. Chop or cutlet bones are perhaps the most dangerous of all, and I make sure no dog ever gets the remains of a mutton chop. It is the splintering that is so dangerous.

If you have provided, as I suggest, a kennel and run unit for your youngster, he can spend part of every day there while you are out, can sleep there at night, and can have his food there. If you have another dog, he can also eat his marrow-bones while they are new in his private run, so that bone-snatching and bullying for beds cannot take place.

Also, a boss dog cannot stop a lesser light from sleeping in bed, or even entering the door of the bedroom, forcing the weaker one to sleep out in the open on bare cement, as often happens if dogs share a bed-compartment, even though it has twin beds.

There are one or two things that have to be watched in the kennel. For instance, the wire of the compound must be absolutely dog-proof, buried underground round the edges and turned over at the top to prevent the dogs jumping out. The gate to the outside world needs a concrete step under it because, as you cannot bury the wire here, it is a potentially weak spot. Although you will find it lovely to put your dogs out in safety for a good play during the day, you will find that Satan still finds some mischief for bone-idle Labradors to do, and after they have played and romped and galloped and dug, they will start tormenting and bothering the older dogs, trying to rile the old stud dog, dig under the fence, or pull a weak place in the wire with their teeth. For this reason I never leave them for hours on end in the compound, but after they start to sit about idly or tease each other I put them back in their double day-runs, friends together, and let them lounge and chew their marrow-bones on the big old kitchen tables with the legs sawn off that I provide in each double run for the purpose. The dogs may also be examined or attended to on these tables when you yourself want to stand upright. Very often I give the older dogs about half an hour in the compound and then put them away, and let the bigger puppies out to romp for an hour or more, until they too start to lie about or prowl around idly. Then back they go, and another lot come out, perhaps the bitches. This is the best way to use a compound; the dogs like this routine and soon get to know it.

With the aid of the kennels and runs, my daily routine for adults is as follows. As early as possible, I let the dogs out of the corral, and take them all for a walk. I then clean out and see to sawdust, straw, water, marrow-bones, puppies' breakfasts etc. Then they either play in the corral, or go back to their double-runs to rest, spending the day like this if not out shooting, showing, having a car ride, shopping, or out for walks or training. Supper is an hour before sunset, followed by a walk. Then at dark, they are put into their night compartments and closed down for the night.

If they are living in kennels like this, I make a point of seeing that the individual dogs get individual attention, and that every dog is made much of, talked to and given a pat whenever I go out. I also give them as many 'treats' as I can manage, such as a run in the car when I go shopping, or an extra and unexpected walk. Boredom is the worst thing possible for a dog.

TEETHING

Having got your dog or dogs into a daily routine, all should now go smoothly for you. The next thing that will happen is that at about four and a half months teething will be in progress. There is nothing much you can do to help this natural process, except that you should have got the inoculation over at three and a half to four months, not later, before teething starts. The puppy will teethe without you knowing much about it, but in spite of this it is a bit of a strain, and you must give the marrow-bones and the calcium, the vitamin D and the Vetzyme (vitamin B). You must also look at intervals to see that the puppy is getting rid of the milk teeth all right and that they are not staying firmly in place, causing a double row of teeth with the milk teeth crowding the growth of the new teeth. If I see a milk tooth sticking, then I get a dentist or vet to remove it. But this seldom happens with Labradors (though often with Terriers), so although you should look out for it, it is unlikely to happen. Nearly always, you will feel the tooth a bit loose and can wobble it a little more each day, giving big bones to chew till it loosens and comes out. I also watch out for the teeth coming wrong and the puppy becoming undershot (the lower teeth protruding beyond the upper). Again, this is not common in Labradors, but it should be watched for at this age, because an undershot bitch should not be bred from, and is useless for show, so there is no point in wasting time rearing and keeping an undershot puppy if you want it as a show dog or foundation bitch. You might as well sell it as a pet–companion at once, without further expense. Cut your losses and start again, although it's sad to have to do this. This teething problem is one of the reasons for paying more for an older puppy.

Early Training

There is no reason why, whilst your puppy is teething, you should not start its hand-training. I am writing a separate chapter on the subject of training, but there are two first steps which come into 'management' and should be taught to every puppy, whatever its purpose, without delay.

These are to 'sit' and 'stay' on command, and to walk on the lead at heel, properly and without pulling. Indeed, you may start the 'sit' lesson as young as you like, provided the puppy is old enough mentally to know it is a serious business and not just a game to be played when it likes and ignored if it suits it.

The method is simple. Get the puppy somewhere where it can't back away from you, and give it a friendly stroke and a kind word to reassure it that you are not going to hurt it. Then very gently take the chin in one hand and place the other hand on its hind-quarters and, gently lifting the chin and pressing the hind-quarters down, say 'Sit' clearly at the same moment. Do this frequently, and the puppy will soon need very little pressing down, so long as you praise him well when he has done it. Gradually you can get him sitting without the chin-lift, and then without the press on his rump. Once he has learnt 'sit' you take him on to 'stay', holding him down in the sitting position while you say 'Stay'. Keep him down with one hand while you raise your finger and hold it up till you are ready to let him up again. Then say 'All right' in an encouraging voice and make much of him to show how clever he is. He will soon learn this as a trick and will enjoy doing his 'stay' exercise. As he progresses, leave him down longer and longer and change the raised finger in his face to a raised hand which will be his final command which you will use all his life. This lesson will eventually be practised while you are out of sight but watching him through a window, or while you walk a distance away from him, and also with a whistle-command added to your raised hand, so that you can sit him and make him stay down at a long distance. This lesson is perhaps the most important of all, and every training step is based on it throughout his life.

One word of warning. Once he gets the idea, he must *never* not sit if you tell him to, and he must stay until you say 'All right'. Never let him get away with disobeying the 'sit' command, even if you have to force him down and hold him for a few seconds. It is a *most* important command, and laxness or careless disobedience must always be dealt with immediately.

Training him to walk properly on the lead is the other important aspect of nursery training and is best taught before he gets too strong. At four to four and a half months old, get a small collar and lead that fits him tightly, and put it on securely. Then set off with him, calling him as you do so. If he loves you, which he should by now, he will set off with you, but will then wander to one side and feel the pull. You will be holding the lead in your *left* hand and firmly pull him on. He will struggle and toss about like a hooked salmon and will somersault and probably yell. Before he gets too desperate, pull him right up to you, slack off the pull and bend down and reassure him. When he has settled again, repeat the process, so that it is drag, struggle, pull up to you, slack off, and pat. In this way the puppy will suddenly cease to struggle and will walk a few steps with you. He will probably start his struggles again, but now each time he will be easier, and you then walk him back towards home when he will start rushing ahead. Pull him right back, and try and make him walk without straining until he reaches his kennel. Give him a good petting while still on the lead, then release him. Try again the next day and you are likely to find that he has got the idea and you will not have more than another minute or two's difficulty.

After he is 'halter-broken', which is what we call the above exercise, the next thing is to teach him to walk without pulling. And I warn you, make sure of this lesson, because when he grows up it will save you from a lot of trouble, aching arms and possibly broken-legged children, wife or granny, who are all too easily pulled over. The lesson is simple to teach, and there is absolutely no need at all for a pulling, scrabbling dog.

Take the lead, as always, in your left hand, and a rolled newspaper or twiggy stick in the other. Walk alongside a wall with the dog on your left and the wall close beyond him on his left side so that he is 'sandwiched'. Say 'Heel' firmly and pull him back behind you on the left so that he walks slightly behind you. As soon as he presses forward so that you see his nose overtaking your left knee, tap him on the nose with the bushy twig or rolled paper. There's no need to hurt or hit him; just force him back to the proper heel position and walk on again. He'll soon learn that if he passes your left knee it means something pushed into his face or a rap on the nose. When he is certain of this, try him in an open place. You can always take him back to the wall-side if he is not yet proficient. Never be afraid to put him back a lesson or two. A refresher is good for him, and he learns better in easy stages. Another successful method is to have the dog on the left as always, but feed his lead behind your back and into your right hand. This means he *cannot* pass your knee because you pull him back into place from behind, your right hand behind your back holding the lead and taking the pull across your back. This works, but I prefer the rolled newspaper or bushy twig method myself, because he withdraws of his own accord, and is not pulled back, as he is with the other method. To me the latter method merely teaches him his correct place at heel but does not teach him not to lean into his lead.

I do advise that this lesson is learnt well. It will certainly pay you dividends to teach him, while he is young enough to be easily controlled, not to pull on the lead and to walk correctly on your left and slightly behind you so that he does not trip you with his foot. You should not leave it until he is stronger than you are, and has already learnt to pull.

One word of warning: do not progress from hand-training to retrieving lessons until the second teeth are fully through and firmly in place. This is because while still teething, a loose tooth may catch in the dummy and cause him pain, which will either put him off his retrieving completely, or cause him to retaliate by biting the offending dummy, which may start the pernicious habit of biting his birds in the future. Do not start his training proper until he is five and a half months old, by which time his teeth should be firmly rooted. (See Chapter 10.)

4 Pedigree and Breed Points

If you have done your homework well and gone to a fair amount of trouble to get a Labrador to suit your purpose, whether for companion, family dog, shooting or Field Trials, you will want to know as it gets older whether it is making up into a good specimen of its breed, and you will also probably be getting interested in its pedigree.

When you first bought the puppy, you should have received the pedigree from the breeder and he or she will have explained the basic essentials, probably showing you the dam of your puppy and telling you the virtues and some of the record of the sire. But other than that, it is probably just a list of unknown names, some underlined in red ink, and after the first glance you may have put the pedigree away in a drawer and forgotten about it. However, sooner or later when out with your Labrador, somebody interested in the breed will come up and say something like 'Who is she?' or 'What is that?' The answer given by the new owner is nearly always 'It's a Labrador,' which is not what we interested people are wanting to know. When we try and delve further, all we can get out of the owner is a vague 'She has got a pedigree as long as your arm.' But by the time the fourth or fifth person has shown interest and tried to find out about the pedigree, then you may start to realise that there is more in a pedigree and to a Labrador than meets the eye.

First let me assure you that there is nothing secret, or exclusive and therefore valuable, about a pedigree. Your dog's registration and sire and dam have been published by the Kennel Club for everyone to read, and anyone can get the pedigree from the Kennel Club, up to five generations, for a small fee, without any authorisation from either the owner or the breeder. Thus there is no value in the piece of paper itself; it is what it contains and how the names in it are arranged that matters.

A pedigree tells experienced breeders a lot of valuable details, and they can spot in a second whether the dog is well-bred (which does not just mean lots of red ink and Champions), and whether the right strains have been put together by a clever breeder or are totally insignificant in that they annul each other instead of complementing each other's virtues. These are the sort of things for which a pedigree is valuable. It is not just a label or certificate of pure breeding, it is the book in which all the inherited factors of the dog are laid out clearly for those who know their bloodlines to see and work with accordingly.

Once you have realised that, a whole new world of Labrador knowledge is opened to you and you can follow up these 'recipes' and bloodlines right back to the beginnings of the Labrador.

At first you may think, like all the general public, that the pedigree should not repeat names more than once, and you may expect fits, mange, nerves and other bad points such as these because you and your friends will consider your dog 'too highly bred'. This is just not true. The dog can only produce what lies in his breeding genetically.

If you breed completely into unrelated bloodlines you are merely building up a reservoir of unknown bad faults (and virtues of course) that you don't know are there, although a good few of them will appear unexpectedly in any resulting puppy. On the other hand, if you have a carefully line-bred pedigree, in which the same name or strain appears more than once, possibly three or four times in a five generation pedigree, then provided the dog whose name is repeated was a good sire, not noted for any bad weakness but showing a lot of positive virtues, then you have every hope of getting at least some of those virtues into your puppy; and if the other names in the pedigree are known for virtues and not bad faults and actually fit in with the dog's virtues and correct any slight faults he may have had, then you have every chance of a puppy better than the parents. Remember that I am speaking about *line-breeding* now, i.e. the collecting of the blood of a dog or strain noted for its virtue, inter-twining it with good unrelated lines also known for similar virtues and if possible opposite to the faults, so that these stand a chance of being corrected (every dog and strain has some faults and the perfect Labrador is still to come). I have not so far been talking about inbreeding (breeding with very close relations), which I consider most undesirable, although I have been forced to resort to it twice. In both cases the bitch refused to allow a strange dog to mate her and would only accept her brother. This I did not like and the results of these two matings were not what I would have wanted on the whole, although there were one or two good puppies.

Genetics

I do not propose to go deeply into genetics here, because the ordinary Labrador breeder only needs to know the most basic genetic facts. I shall put these into simple language, seeing that this book is largely written for beginners and novices; genetics can be more dangerous than of use if they are understood imperfectly.

So I shall be dealing here only with the simplest working of

A. COMPLETE OUTCROSS PEDIGREE No dogs appear twice –
No dog related to another.

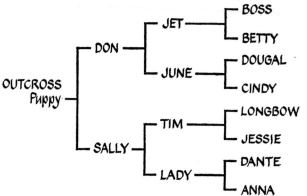

B. LINE-BRED PEDIGREE to BOSS (three times), chosen because he
was a good influence on the breed.

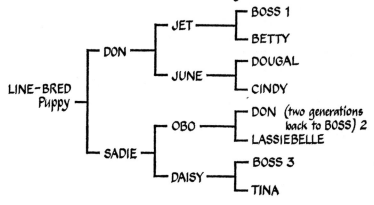

C. IN-BRED PEDIGREE No fresh blood introduced – thus doubling
on faults and virtues.

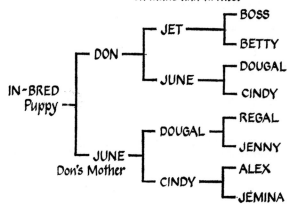

Fig 2
Complete Outcross,
Line-Bred and In-
Bred Pedigrees

dominant over recessive genes as proved by Mendel in his famous and important experiment with peas.

Briefly, he found that there were two factors controlling each characteristic, one dominant and one recessive. He found that this theory, of which I give a chart, worked with other living creatures and appeared to be a primary law of nature, as is accepted today.

The basic facts are these: many inherited traits, such as colour, length of coat and legs, eye-colour and many others are ruled by genes which the dog inherits from the parents.

(1) The dominant always over-rules the recessive. For example, in Labradors, black is dominant over yellow, therefore over-rules it. This means that if a dog possesses the *black* gene in his make-up (please note that throughout, this refers to genetic make-up, and *not* necessarily the colour of his sire or dam), then he himself is *always black*.

(2) If he possesses the recessive gene for yellow, he can still be black himself (indeed most Blacks possess the yellow gene) but can pass on the yellow recessive to his children, producing Yellow puppies.

(3) *All* Yellows, however bred, and they may have two black parents and four black grandparents, are completely without any black genes (or they would automatically be black themselves, black genes always over-ruling yellow genes).

So as my chart points out, pure-dominant Blacks mated together do not contain any yellow and therefore cannot pass them on, their puppies always being black. These pure-dominant Blacks are unable to produce Yellows whatever the circumstances.

● Pure-dominant Black, carrying NO yellow gene.

◐ Impure Black, i.e. coloured black but carrying the gene for yellow.

◑ Yellow, carrying no black gene whatever the parental colouring

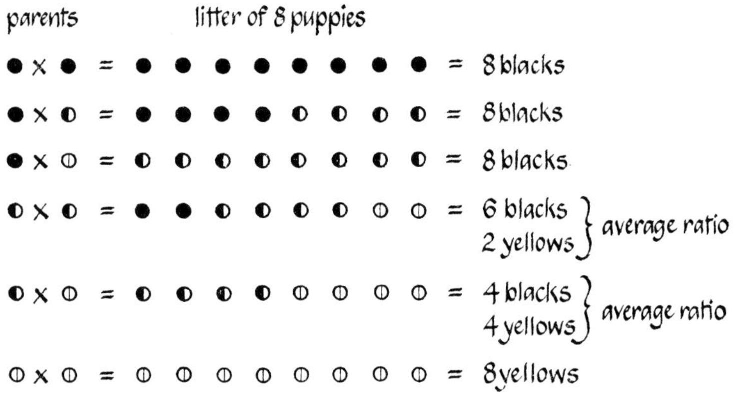

parents   litter of 8 puppies

● × ● = ● ● ● ● ● ● ● ● = 8 blacks

● × ◐ = ● ● ● ● ◐ ◐ ◐ ◐ = 8 blacks

● × ◑ = ◐ ◐ ◐ ◐ ◐ ◐ ◐ ◐ = 8 blacks

◐ × ◐ = ● ● ◐ ◐ ◐ ◐ ◑ ◑ = 6 blacks } average ratio
     2 yellows

◐ × ◑ = ◐ ◐ ◐ ◐ ◑ ◑ ◑ ◑ = 4 blacks } average ratio
     4 yellows

◑ × ◑ = ◑ ◑ ◑ ◑ ◑ ◑ ◑ ◑ = 8 yellows

Fig 3
Colour chart showing the workings of a dominant over recessive

Impure Blacks, which are themselves black but which carry the recessive yellow gene, can produce both colours, provided they are not mated to the above-mentioned pure-dominant Blacks.

Yellow mated to an impure Black can produce Yellows and Blacks (although Yellow, if mated to a pure-dominant Black, is completely over-ruled, and cannot then produce any Yellows at all).

Lastly, and most important, two Yellows mated together contain no black genes whatsoever (even though they may *both* come from black parents). Because of this total lack of black genes (which is proved by the fact they themselves are yellow, because if either contained the black gene it would automatically be black itself), the product of two Yellows is *always* yellow. So when mating two Yellows together, even though the parents and grandparents are all Blacks don't think that you will breed yourself some nice black puppies from this Yellow × Yellow mating, because you won't. Or if you do, then you can be certain the litter is not by the yellow dog. To produce black puppies from a yellow bitch the dog *must himself* be black.

On the other hand, as I have already said, two Blacks may produce Yellows if they *both* carry the yellow gene, but should one of these blacks happen to be a pure Black and contain no yellow gene, then that pure Black can *never* produce Yellows however he is mated. A famous example of this was Ch. Whatstandwell Ballyduff Robin who never produced a yellow puppy to any bitch whatever her colour or however bred. My own Cora of Mansergh (the dam of my Ch. Midnight of Mansergh) never produced a Yellow. They were pure-dominant Blacks and did not inherit a yellow gene although their pedigrees contained yellow ancestors.

This explanation of colour inheritance shows the actual workings of the simple dominant–recessive theory; it acts for *any* faults or virtues which are known to be dominant or recessive. There are further complications when other factors are brought in, such as the liver colour, the working of which in relation to black and yellow would take two pages of 'algebra' to explain. For this reason I cannot embark upon Livers (Chocolates) because there are several different sorts of liver, all acting differently. All that the ordinary Labrador breeder knows about it, unless a genetics expert or colour specialist, is that it is difficult to breed a good dark Liver with the correct-coloured eyes, that few have done it to date, and that it is the most difficult colour to prognosticate. Because of this, breeding Livers has always been difficult and chancy, and to date in this country there have only been three Liver Champions.

IS YOUR LABRADOR A GOOD SPECIMEN OF THE BREED?
To help you here there is an official Kennel Club Standard. This can be obtained by writing to the Kennel Club, whose address is given in

A beautiful young bitch typifying quality and activity. Ch. Damson of Mansergh.

the Appendix. They will send you a copy for a small sum. It is well worth the money. If you have joined a Labrador breed club, which I strongly advise (there are breed clubs covering all parts of Britain, a list of which is also in the Appendix) then the Secretary will send you a copy on request, and it may also be published in the Year Book, certainly in the Labrador Club's Year Book and also the Midland Counties Labrador Club Year Book.

Briefly the Standard says that a Labrador should be:

1 Strongly built, short-coupled, and very active. Broad in the skull, broad and deep through chest and ribs, broad and strong over the loins and hind-quarters. The coat must be close, short, with dense weather-resisting undercoat, free from feather or wave, giving a fairly hard feeling to the hand.

2 Skull broad with pronounced 'stop' so that the skull is not in a straight line with the nose. Head clean-cut without fleshy cheeks. Jaws of medium length and powerful, free from snipiness. Nose wide, nostrils well developed. Eyes medium-sized, intelligent and good tempered, brown or hazel in colour. Teeth strong and sound,

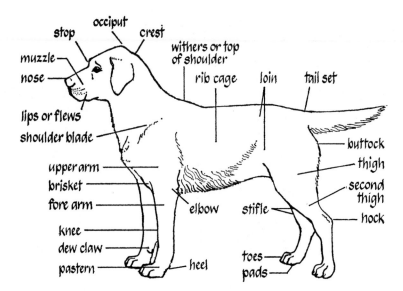

Fig 4
The Points of the
Labrador

the lower teeth just behind but touching the upper. Ears should not be large or heavy and should hang close to the head, set rather far back.

3 Neck clean, strong, powerful, set into well-placed shoulders, which should be long and sloping. The forelegs well boned and straight from shoulder to ground either from the front view or the side view. The movement must be neither too wide nor too close in front.

4 The body should be of good width and depth, ribs well sprung; back short-coupled.

5 The hind-quarters must have wide strong loins, the stifles well sprung, the hind-quarters well developed and not sloping towards the tail. The hocks slightly bent, not cow-hocked, moving neither too wide nor too close behind.

6 The feet should be round and compact, toes well arched and pads well developed. The tail should be very thick towards the base, gradually tapering to the tip, of medium length, practically free from feathering, and clothed all round with the Labrador's short, thick, dense coat, giving a peculiar rounded appearance known as 'otter tail'. The tail may be carried gaily but should not curl over the back. Colour generally black or yellow, other whole colours being permitted. The coat should be free from white markings, except that a small white spot on the chest is allowable. The coat should be whole-coloured and not of flecked appearance.

7 The desired height is: dogs, 22–22½ in; bitches, 21½–22 in., measured from the shoulder or withers vertically to the ground by the forefoot, just as you measure a horse.

Above Left: A correct Labrador front, straight and true. Sh. Ch. Balrion King Frost. *Above Right*: A beautiful Labrador head and expression. Eastview Topper of Mansergh. *Left*: Excellent hind-quarters, tail-set and stance. Sh. Ch. Crawcrook Princess.

Of course the Standard does not and cannot describe type, nor does it attempt to go deeply into conformation. It does not say that a Labrador should have two eyes and four legs. This is taken as already known and understood. Nor does it say that there should not be a ewe-neck or that the dog should not have string-halt or sickle-hocks. These are things that a judge is expected to know for himself. The correct anatomy of a dog is left for the breeder to find out for himself.

While anatomy may be learned from books, type is a difficult thing to learn in Labradors, with no help from the Standard, because it cannot be described. It can only be learned by looking at Labradors, looking at photographs of famous dogs past and present, and by getting other Labrador people to point out good typical Labradors to you in their kennels or at shows.

One of the reasons for the differing types we see at shows is that different breeders interpret the Standard rather differently and therefore breed slightly different Labradors. But the correct type is well known to most good breeders and can be shown to the interested novice, so they can eventually evaluate type for themselves.

I have tried to help here by selecting the photographs for this book very carefully, so that you have a chance to see good typical Labradors and get the type into your eye.

Some Possible Dogs in Your Pedigree

In this section, I describe some well-known dogs and kennels which may appear in your pedigree.

At any time there will be in this country four or five outstanding famous and fashionable dogs, and also perhaps the same number of famous bitches. There will also be several famous 'recipes', i.e. a certain dog mated to a certain bitch may suddenly come up trumps and will produce a batch of top-class puppies, outstanding in every way. To give an example of this, which we call a 'nick', I will mention the 'Tan–Shadow mating', as it is known in Labradors, and from which it is pretty sure your own Labrador will descend, probably several times. Australian Ch. Sandylands Tan (before he went out to Australia), twice mated a black bitch called Sandylands Shadow. Mrs Gwen Broadley was the breeder of these two litters, and owner of both sire and dam.

The results of these two litters were 'nicks', providing many Champions and overseas Champions, several of these being famous sires in their own right. The great Ch. Sandylands Tandy was one of these, the two litters also containing Ch. Sandylands Tanya, Ch. Sandylands Truth (a famous dam), Ch. Sandylands Tanna, several overseas Ch.s, and Reanacre Sandylands Tarmac, who won a Res. C.C. on the bench and also prizes at Field Trials. This must be one of

Ch. Sandylands
Truth, a famous
brood bitch.

the most famous and influential 'nicks' of all times, and it is difficult to
find a good pedigree that does not contain this famous mating,
probably several times.

All the dogs and bitches that follow have had a tremendous influence
and are still doing so in the present day in Labradors. Many are still
alive as I write in autumn 1979.

Pride of place as an influence must go to Ch. Sandylands Mark, the
record-holder in any breed for the number of British Champion
children he sired here: twenty-six to date, not to mention his
innumerable Champion children overseas. His influence is still hard at
work today, and your pedigree is almost certain to contain his name,
especially if it contains Black bloodlines.

Ch. Sandylands Mark was an extremely sturdy, strongly built,
medium-sized black dog. He had the kindest of expressions, a
charming head and a really stout, well-ribbed body. He was short-
coupled and barrel-ribbed and had an extremely dense, strong double
coat. He had a splendid otter tail, thick round the base, short and
straight. Mark was noted for strong bone all through, but especially in
his leg bone. He stood on good feet, and had really no weaknesses,
which is probably why he was so strong in his tremendous influence on
any sort of bitch that visited him. He was the kindest, nicest dog.
Gwen Broadley loved him dearly till the day of his death at a ripe old
age. He holds the record for the number of British Championship progeny
he sired, and through them and their progeny, he breeds on to this day.

Ch. Midnight of Mansergh, progenitor in a line of six generations of Mansergh Champions. Also sire of sixteen award winners at Field Trials.

Behind the Yellow bloodlines lie the tremendous influences of Ch. Braeduke Joyful, Ch. Diant Swandyke Cream Cracker and Ch. Landyke Lancer. These were three splendid Yellows, grand dogs of strength and soundness. Also behind many pedigrees lies the grand Yellow, Dual Ch. Staindrop Saighdear. Although these dogs will have had a great influence on your Yellow lines, I am not going to describe them at length, because they will lie so far back that they will not appear in your own pedigree, even though some of them will be there behind it, as may the Black dogs Ch. Reanacre Mallardhurn Thunder (Ch. S. Mark's father), Ch. Midnight of Mansergh, Ch. Holton Baron, and Ch. Ruler of Blaircourt (Tweed's father). These are the distant dogs appearing well behind your pedigree.

Likely to appear in the first four columns will be the following, all of which I describe from my own knowledge of them, having competed against all of them.

Ch. Poolstead Problem. A grand Yellow dog, very strongly built and sound. He has a lovely head with a very good, dignified, yet kind, expression. Well-proportioned, with good coat and tail-set and a nice otter tail, he has good bone and feet, and is a most regal-looking dog of nice temperament.

Ch. Follytower Merrybrook Black Stormer is having a great influence, not only on the Black bloodlines, but is also notable for siring two of the only three Chocolate Champions there have yet been in this country. He himself is a great favourite with the public, a great ambassador for the breed with his cheerful friendly disposition and his showmanship, which never flags. He stands looking up at his owner in show-stance, wagging his tail, alert and intelligent throughout. Stormer has tremendous presence, and a nice head set on to a long

Sh. Ch. Poolstead Problem.

powerful neck which adds tremendous finish to his appearance. He is of graceful proportions and looks so very attractive in the ring. Standing on good legs and feet, Stormer's tail is particularly well carried, straight off his back-line. He is a most powerful influence on the Chocolates to date, both here and in America, where his son Ch. Lawnwoods Hot Chocolate is making a great name as a sire. Stormer is also having a big influence on Black lines everywhere both in his own right and also through his great son, Ch. Sandylands Storm-Along, of whom more later.

Ch. Ballyduff Marketeer. A grand Black son of Ch. Mark's, Marketeer is built on much the same lines as Mark, though perhaps a

Ch. Follytower Merrybrook Black Stormer, a great black sire and the leading influence in Chocolates. Photo taken at the age of ten years.

shade longer in the leg. He is a striking Black, with good head and expression, strong bone and excellent outline. He is proving a great influence on the Black bloodlines all over the world, with many good progeny to different types of bitches. Like all the Ballyduffs, there is a strong influence for work in Marketeer, this strain being a true dual-purpose bloodline. Ch. Marketeer produced Ch. Squire of Ballyduff, a neat shapely Black who is a Ch. on the showbench and also a winner at Trials and a most attractive dog, neat and sweet.

Ch. Nokeener Taffy is a big, strong-boned dog, a really grand up-standing Yellow with a tremendous influence, especially in Wales and the surrounding country. He has a grand head, a good neck with excellent shoulders, a strong body with a good rib-cage, and strong hind-quarters. He is having an excellent influence on both Black and Yellow lines, and seems to do good on any type of bitch. With the remoteness of some of the Welsh Labrador kennels from the good English dogs, he gets all sorts and sizes of bitches with many different bloodlines, and seems to be able to improve on any bitch that comes to him, being such a strong, powerful, excellent dog himself.

Ch. Balrion King Frost. A medium-sized, very compact Black of most charming character. Like Stormer, he stands in beautiful show-stance looking up at his handler with the most pleasing expression. He stands on good legs and feet with an excellent coat and short otter tail. King Frost is noted for his appearance of health and well-being, and is tremendously popular with the ringside, always 'asking for', and very often getting, the top award. A great ambassador for the breed, and a kind, polite, most charming Black dog.

International Ch. Lawnwoods Hot Chocolate, a Chocolate dog now in America, is a son of Stormer, and is having a tremendous influence on the Chocolates in both countries. He is renowned for his smartest-of-smart outline and stance, showing all the time for all he is worth. A most striking dog of splendid colour, with long neck and good shoulders, excellent back-line and stance, he always looks so keen and braced and ready to go anywhere with his soundness and activity. He is the principal influence in Chocolates in America.

Sh. Ch. Sandylands Storm-Along. Perhaps the greatest blow the breed has ever suffered is the loss of this splendid young Black dog even before he was fully matured. In his short show career, he had been meteoric, the top judges of Labradors appreciating his worth at once and, most fortunately (and, I must add, astutely) sending their very top bitches to him. He had served two Champion bitches among the very first bitches to visit him, a signal honour for such a young dog. Funnily enough he was not a very popular dog with the ringsiders, perhaps because he went so high so very young, and therefore they could not see his tremendous virtues through his immaturity, because he was a slow developer. But the virtues were there for the knowledgeable to see, and so he had the very best bitches. From these he sired some really splendid puppies, full of quality and excellence. Sadly he died before he was three, but his influence is already there, and his name made. Although he died so young and had comparatively few bitches to him, his influence is enormously for the good and will last for a long time.

Ch. Timspring Sirius is a very active shapely Black. He is a willing, alert, intelligent dog, and again a great ambassador in the show ring with his intelligent head and expression. Like Stormer and King Frost, Sirius loves the show ring and shows for all he is worth. A happy, kind dog, in full co-operation with his owner Mrs Macan.

It is very much more difficult to pinpoint the great bitches of the present day, because their fame is very often due entirely to a mating to one dog that proved to be a 'nick'. Behind most of the pedigrees of today, though now too far behind to appear in your written pedigree, will certainly lie *Sandylands Shadow,* not a Champion herself, but a very pleasant nicely made Black who, mated to Aust. Ch. Sandylands Tan (who was never a Champion in this country, but again a very pleasant extremely nice Yellow), produced that great batch of Champions in her two litters, which themselves have influenced every winning bloodline all over the world. As I have previously said, this mating has been perhaps the most important to the Labrador breed of any. Shadow will certainly lie behind your pedigree, probably several times.

Braeduke Julia of Poolstead was another great bitch, this time a Yellow, a big, handsome, roomy bitch, as a good brood should be. The Poolstead foundation bitch, her influence lies behind most of the

Ch. Braeduke Julia of Poolstead with two of her children, Ch. Poolstead Powderpuff (left) and Sh. Ch. Poolstead President (right).

Ch. Ballyduff Holly-branch of Keithray.

numerous Yellow Champions produced at Poolstead, a tremendously powerful line of good Champion brood bitches. She herself, in five litters to four different stud dogs, produced no less than four English Champions, and one American Champion.

The Black *Ch. Hollybank Beauty* is another that, mated twice to Ch. Sandylands Tweed of Blaircourt, could not go wrong. These two matings produced the famous Holly Champions, the breeder being Mrs Wilkinson of the Keithray prefix. *Ch. Ballyduff Hollybranch of Keithray* lies behind the all-powerful Ballyduffs of today, and thus his dam, Ch. Hollybank Beauty, appears behind nearly all the Black pedigrees of today.

Ch. Hollybank Beauty herself was a most lovely Black bitch, just the sort to make a brood bitch, roomy and scopey, yet with all the true Labrador essentials, perhaps the most lovely bitch I have ever seen. She had a curious story behind her fame. Bred by Mrs Pauling of the Cookridge strain, one Sunday afternoon the Wilkinsons went to Cookridge to buy a puppy for their son Keith's birthday. Mrs Pauling was out with the dogs and Mr Pauling, not realising that a puppy had been 'selected' from the litter, showed the puppies to the Wilkinsons. With their great Yorkshire eye (Yorkshiremen seem notable in their ability to pick the very best of anything) Mrs Wilkinson picked out one puppy, although she then knew next to nothing about Labradors. Her eye did not play her false, and when Mrs Pauling returned, there was young Keith Wilkinson hugging her 'selected' puppy as his own. Mrs Pauling was horrified; she had never had any intention of selling this bitch, but the deed was done, and with a small boy involved she hadn't the heart to take the precious puppy away from him. So Hollybank Beauty became the property of Keith Wilkinson. But this curious story did not end there.

The Wilkinsons had a caravan somewhere near Morecambe and when on holiday there they went into the local butcher to buy their meat; their 'pet' was spotted by an astute English Setter breeder who happened to be shopping too. She was amazed at the beauty of the bitch and said that the Wilkinsons simply *must* show her. So that was how possibly the most lovely Black bitch of all time came into the picture and through the Tweed and Beauty matings, her influence remains for all time.

A famous brood bitch, Mandy of Breakneck Farm.

Other great influences in the bitch line in present day pedigrees were *Ch. Diant Juliet,* a gorgeous Yellow bitch on lovely Labrador lines, her daughter *Diant Pride* (who, being the mother of Sandylands Shadow, lies behind the great Tan–Shadow nick), *Electron of Ardmargha,* whose mating to Int. Ch. Ballyduff Seaman had such an influence on the Ballyduff lines, and *Mandy of Breakneck Farm,* who lies behind the great Rookwood Champions, being the Rookwood foundation bitch.

While I am able to name and describe present-day famous *dogs*, it is much more difficult to give the great *dams* actually living today. They are probably only mated three or four times in their lifetimes, often less, and their influence only shows when their progeny become Champions and in their turn make their mark. Their fame lies in the future and their descendants, so I cannot prophesy their influence yet. Time alone will tell.

5 The Origins of the Labrador

Although a lot of research has been done on the origins of the Labrador, there is still no concrete evidence as to how the Labrador arose, or where he came from originally.

We do know that Colonel Peter Hawker saw them in Newfoundland in 1814, describing them as the St John's Breed of Newfoundland, a variety of the true Newfoundland. He said that the St John's variety was the 'best for every kind of shooting; he is generally black and no bigger than a Pointer, with very fine legs, smooth short hair, does not carry his tail so much curled as the other and is extremely quick running, swimming and fighting.' According to Colonel Hawker, the proper Labrador was very large, strong of limb with rough hair, and carried his tail very high (all these nineteenth-century writers use the words Newfoundland and Labrador indiscriminately, as also the words Retriever and Spaniel).

W. E. Cormack, who lived for some time in St John's, says the St John's Labradors were 'small water-dogs, admirably trained as retrievers in fowling and are otherwise useful.' He goes on to say that 'the smooth or short-coated dog is preferred in frosty weather; the long-coated kind become encumbered with the ice on coming out of the water.'

Colonel Hawker says, when talking about pheasant shooting in covert, 'We rarely see a Pointer, however expert in fetching his birds, that will follow up the scent of, and find the wounded ones, half so well as the real St John's Newfoundland dogs.'

Edward Jesse, Esq. (as he styles himself on the title-page of his 1858 book *Anecdotes of Dogs*), in his chapter headed 'The Newfoundland Dog', quotes from *Excursions in and about Newfoundland* by Jukes. The passage reads:

'A thin short-haired black dog belonging to George Harvey came off to us today; this animal was of a breed very different from what we understand by the term Newfoundland dog in England. He had a thin tapering snout, a long thin tail, and rather thin but powerful legs, with a lank body, the hair short and smooth. These are the most abundant dogs of the country, the long-haired curly dogs being comparatively rare. They are by no means handsome, but are generally more intelligent and useful than the others.

'This one caught his own fish; he sat on a projecting rock beneath a fish-lake or stage, where the fish are laid to dry, watching the water, which had a depth of six or eight feet, the bottom of which was white with fish-bones. On throwing a piece of codfish into the water, three or four heavy clumsy-looking fish, called in Newfoundland "sculpins", with great heads and mouths, and many spines about them and generally about a foot long, would swim in to catch it. These he would "set" attentively, and the moment one turned his broadside to him, he darted down like a fish-hawk, and seldom came up without the fish in his mouth. As he caught them he carried them regularly to a place a few yards off where he laid them down, and they told us that in the summer he would sometimes make a pile of fifty or sixty a day just at that place.

'He never attempted to eat them, but seemed to be fishing purely for his own amusement. I watched him for about two hours, and when the fish did not come I observed he once or twice put his right foot in the water and paddled it about. The foot was white and Harvey said he did it to toll or entice the fish; but whether it was for that specific reason, or merely a motion of impatience, I could not exactly decide.'

From these writings by Colonel Hawker, W. E. Cormack and Mr Jukes, it seems that all three considered there to be *three* 'Newfoundlands', the 'true breed, the Labrador and the St John's'. The answer is that the St John's Labrador and the St John's Newfoundland is one and the same dog, whoever describes it, and that by all these descriptions he is the identical dog that we know as the Labrador today. The breed was there exactly as we know it except for size, which varied in different accounts and was obviously not settled; the type, coat, tail and the sporting and retrieving ability were all ready-made and established by the time these travellers arrived to describe them.

Where or how did these dogs get there, on the bleak Newfoundland coast? Lord George Scott and Sir John Middleton in *The Labrador Dog, its Home and History* (1936), came to the conclusion that they were descendants of a medley of dogs, pure and cross-bred, that came over with the fishermen from Devon who settled there to fish the Cod Banks.

This theory seems to me to be extremely unlikely, although local dogs may have played a small part in the evolution of the Labrador as a distinct breed. One of the inconsistencies in this theory is that it is difficult enough to breed a pure black dog without large white patches from a line of pedigree dogs, as the Whippet people know, white mis-markings often appearing from their broken-coloured ancestry. I feel that the fisherfolk of Newfoundland, who were busy people living a hard life in a harsh climate, would scarcely bother with breeding out the different points of their various breeds of dogs from Devon so as to produce a whole-coloured dog possessing such distinct and deep-rooted characteristics as did the lesser or St John's Labrador when seen by Colonel Hawker, W. E. Cormack and Mr Jukes.

I have long had an idea that the Labrador probably descends from a Portuguese utility working dog used by farmers in North-West Portugal and the Spanish Border, called the Cane di Castro Laboreiro, which very much resembles a 'bad' Labrador, having many points in common: the same coat and often the same tail, a very similar head and expression, ear-carriage, legs and feet. In particular the thighs are the same shape, a telling point when looking for type and purity in a Labrador.

It seems much more likely to me that the Portuguese, who were a seafaring race, brought these dogs with them when their boats travelled up to the Cod Banks, and that this could account for the coat, tail, head and general appearance, all distinctive in the Labrador and inheritable, which indicates purity of bloodline. These were probably crossed with the Eskimo type of dog that was found around the Northern shores of Canada. It would also account for the name of the Labrador, which could very easily be a corruption of the word 'Laboreiro' if used by the illiterate fishermen of Newfoundland, who would find difficulty in getting their tongues round such an awkward foreign word, but who already knew the word Labrador, it being their neighbouring province.

I am told by someone that travels regularly through the northern border between Portugal, Spain and France that the local dogs working the cattle still look exactly like poor specimens of Labradors, and that at first he believed them to be bad Labradors, until he found them to be the working dog of the district and of ancient descent.

However, we shall never really know where the Labrador came from, apparently ready-made and absolutely distinctive, with many decades of careful breeding for special characteristics such as love of water and children, extreme cleverness at following wounded game, and strong retrieving instincts.

That wonderful author and naturalist William Henry Hudson (1841–1922) writes in his book *Far Away and Long Ago* (1918) of a dog which sounds very like a Labrador. Hudson was at the time of the incident described living in the Pampas of Buenos Aires Province, and was aged six. He tells of the death of an old dog, Caesar, at the age of thirteen. He says: 'Caesar was an old, valued dog, although of no superior breed. He was just an ordinary dog of the country, short-haired with long legs and blunt muzzle.' He goes on to say that

Caesar was about a third larger than the ordinary native cur and was 'as much above all the other dogs of the house, numbering about twelve or fourteen, in intelligence and courage as in size.' Further on Hudson says, 'He was a black dog, now in his old age sprinkled with white hairs all over his body, the face and legs having gone quite grey.' Apparently, 'Caesar could be a terrible fellow in a rage, was an accomplished fighter (see Colonel Hawker's description of a Labrador) or when driving cattle was a terrible being. With us children he was mild tempered and patient, allowing us to ride on his back.'

Sadly enough, Caesar's last years were very wretched. He grew 'irritable and gaunt with his big ribs protruding', this last illness being caused by his teeth: 'They opened his mouth to show us his teeth, big blunt canines and old molars worn down to stumps.' As it was not the custom of the country to put an old dog down, poor Caesar was left to die, although the children who loved him much 'tried to comfort him with warm rugs, food and drink in the sheltered place where he lay, unable to stand up.' Luckily for him he died that night, and was accorded a very solemn funeral conducted with due reverence and with a short sermon on life and death of dogs and Mortal Man, which impressed the six-year-old William Hudson as nothing had ever impressed him before.

At no time does W. H. Hudson suggest that this dog came from foreign climes, but the description so exactly fits a Labrador (note the hair was short and black and did what in old age all Labradors do if of proper true breeding, i.e. 'sprinkling' all over with white hairs and going grey in face and muzzle and legs). To me everything about this dog says 'Labrador', and if not then I would wager that Caesar was descended from the Portuguese utility dog the Cane di Castro Laboreiro, if not actually one of this working cattle-herding breed itself.

So far I have been speaking of the possible sources of the breed in Newfoundland. The advent of the breed to England and Scotland is well known. The first Labradors turned up in the Poole Harbour area in the 1820s, coming over frequently with the cod-boats from Newfoundland. Many missed the boat back and hung about the town and waterfront, as Labradors do to this day in Newfoundland. (Lady Barlow of Newfoundland has sent over photos showing them on the quays and boat-decks of Newfoundland.)

The Poole Harbour Labradors were infused into various English Retriever bloodlines, as a few sporting gentlemen realised their value as shooting and wildfowling dogs. They then more or less died out, until the advent of Buccleuch Avon, who is the ancestor of all Black Labrador strains today. He was a lovely dog, absolutely typical, with a splendid head, the kindest of expressions, a tremendous double coat, and thick-rooted otter tail. Above all, his muzzle, nostrils and the shape of his skull were excellent. He also had good bone running right down into his feet. Whelped in 1885, he was bred by Lord Malmesbury, who had kept his strain of Labradors at Hurn Court near Poole Harbour 'as pure as possible'. He gave the 6th Duke of Buccleuch not only Avon, but also Ned and Nell. To Lord Home he gave Dinah, June and Smut. Buccleuch Avon was sired by Tramp out of Lord Malmesbury's June (1882). The advent of Buccleuch Avon was the most important date in the history of the Labrador. How I wish he were here today, because I would certainly be sending my bitches to him to get that head and expression, coat, tail, type and bone.

Other important Labradors in the history of the breed were the Duke of Hamilton's Sam and Diver, Sir Frederick Graham's Keilder, and Mr Montague Guest's Sankey. This handful of Labradors is recognised as the foundation and rootstock of the Labrador today, with Buccleuch Avon taking pride of place.

There is a beautiful photograph of the 11th Earl of Home's Nell taken as an old bitch in 1867, who, like Avon, is the perfect example of Labrador type, with the same lovely expression, kind and dignified, excellent bone, muzzle and nostrils, skull, ear-carriage, coat and tail. Avon and Nell put to shame our modern Foxhounds, Dobermanns, Boxers, Rottweilers, Great Danes and Bull-Mastiffs that appear masquerading as Labradors today, and get put up as such. (I will be accused of turning the clock back a hundred years. How I wish I could!)

However, to cheer myself and other breeders of the true Labrador type, there are still just enough of these true Labradors (and, thank goodness, a handful of judges who still know and recognise the type), for us to be able to carry on against the flood of wrong sorts, even although we all – breeders, judges and true Labradors – are getting fewer and further between.

I beg of new breeders and judges to turn to the books which contain illustrations of these early dogs so as to know and recognise Labrador type when they see it. I recommend several books that contain splendid examples of the Labradors of long ago, of right types and expression, coat and tail, and ask you to look at the photos in Helen Warwick's *The Complete Labrador*, particularly that on page 37 showing Stellashaw Nell and her son Brayton Sir Richard, absolutely correct in type and identical with those few true Labradors that are being shown today. Lorna Countess Howe's book, *The Popular Labrador Retriever*, has a wonderful head study of Dual Ch. Banchory Bolo, a most beautiful head and expression, which should be the ultimate aim of us all, and a lovely study of 'a typical Munden head'. How anyone can prefer the square, boxy, hard heads and expressions of today I cannot think. If we could get back to this head, we might have less talk of bad temperaments than we breeders are constantly faced with. *Show Dogs* by Theo Marples F.Z.S. also has an excellent specimen representing the Labrador, drawn by Arthur Wardle. This dog is unnamed, but is extremely typical in every way. (Indeed, I am astonished to have bred a dog last year who is the image of this particular dog; I am very happy to have him.)

Other famous dogs and bitches, if you can be lucky enough to find photos of them, are the famous Flapper (the dog who by his prowess in the field turned the shooting men's fancy from Flatcoats, who up to that time had been the most popular Retrievers, to Labradors); Ch. Abbess of Harpotts (my ideal of a Labrador bitch); Ch. Ilderton Ben (held up to me by Lady Howe as the best Labrador ever bred, surprisingly, considering how her devotion to her own Bolo was unshakeable). Lady Howe mentioned Ch. Manor House Belle as the greatest bitch she had seen at that time, saying in her book that she wished she could have compared Ch. Manor House Belle and Ch. Judith Aikshaw, whom she rated the best post-World-War 11 bitch. There have only been ten Dual Champions (correct title Ch. and F.T.Ch.) in this country, these being Banchory Bolo, Banchory Sunspeck, Titus of Whitmore and his son Flute of Flodden, Bramshaw Bob, Banchory Painter, Staindrop Saighdear, Rockstead Footspark, Knaith Banjo, and the only bitch ever to gain this difficult Dual title, Lochar Nessie. Of these ten, eight were Blacks and two Yellows. Buccleuch Avon was the ancestor in direct tail-male line of Bolo, Bob, Saighdear, Banjo and Nessie.

Netherby Boatswain's list of descendants in tail-male contains both Titus and Flute. Smiler's descendants number among them Sunspeck, Painter and Footspark.

It will be seen from this analysis of the tail-male lines of the ten Dual Champions that they trace back to three rootstocks, Avon, Boatswain and Smiler. There is undoubted food for thought here, as there are about seven known tail-male foundation ancestors, and two or three unclassified winner-producing lines who got the odd winner but nothing to compare with the known classified lines, i.e. Lord Malmesbury's Tramp, Netherby Boatswain, Lord Malmesbury's Sweep, Smiler, Mint, Buccleuch Bachelor, Sweep, and the few non-classified lines. All present-day Labradors descend in tail-male from one of these ancestors, with Tramp (through Buccleuch Avon) being by far the best dual-purpose sire. Mr Mackay Sanderson, who did all this research, held very firmly to this statement, and I fully agree with him. He was a remarkable man, knowing more about bloodlines of all the Retriever breeds than anyone else before or since.

Yellow Labradors

Hyde Ben (or Ben of Hyde as he sometimes appears in pedigrees) was the first *registered* Yellow Labrador, coming from two Black parents, Neptune and Duchess, but I have given two reproductions of pictures hanging in that excellent Museum at Barnard Castle, Co. Durham, the Bowes Museum. A visit here is almost a pilgrimage for any Labrador enthusiast, because hanging in the main hall, in the place of honour, is a portrait in oils of Mrs Bowes with, at her side, an absolutely typical Yellow 'Labrador' called Bernadine; I think that there can be no doubt whatsoever that this was a Labrador, it being exactly like the best Yellow Labradors of today. Indeed it is difficult to believe that this dog was not added to the portrait afterwards, it is so modern in looks, but this is completely disproved by another portrait of Bernadine in her yard, which was painted in the late 1840s. As the portrait of Mrs Bowes and Bernadine was painted about the same time, this must be the earliest portrait of a true Yellow we have. The type is quite remarkable, and this dog would not look amiss in the show ring today.

The Bowes Museum is easily accessible, and everyone interested in Labrador history should not fail to pay it a visit, just to see these two portraits of a yellow Labrador painted 130 years ago.

Right: Mrs Josephine Bowes's Yellow bitch Bernadine, by Antoine Dury, which with the portrait of her owner, hangs in Bowes Museum.

Left: Miss Simmond's Ch. Sam of Suddie. Note the close resemblance in type to Bernadine 125 years earlier.

6 How to Show your Labrador

If your puppy is now turned 6 months old, which is the age at which it becomes eligible for the show ring, and if it is reasonably well-grown, in good condition, good-looking and follows the official Breed Standard fairly closely, you may want to try it out in the ring.

If you are just trying it out for a bit of fun, the thing to do is to enter it at a small local show or match-meeting. Find out from a local dog-breeder or pet-shop where the next fairly local show is going to be held and where you should apply for a schedule and entry form. Then find your Registration Certificate for the dog, which unless you registered it yourself should have been handed over at the time of purchase by the breeder or vendor.

If that Certificate is in order, you must also make sure that the puppy has been transferred into your name at the Kennel Club, because it cannot be shown in your name unless the transfer has been sent to the Kennel Club before the date of the show. A dog has to have been registered and transferred correctly before the actual date of the show. If you find that your puppy has not been registered, then do so at once, whereupon you may enter your puppy in the name you have chosen with the letters N.A.F. (Name Applied For) after its name. Remember a name *must* be given. It is no good just writing the letters N.A.F. on the entry form, because the Kennel Club will not accept this. So remember to give the name applied for, *before* the letters N.A.F.

If you find the dog has never been transferred into your name, send the transfer form to the K.C. at once and put the dog's registered name and the letters T.A.F. (Transfer Applied For) on the entry form. Thus your puppy's name may appear on the entry form as (1) 'Black Jack', (2) 'Black Jack N.A.F.', or (3) 'Black Jack N.A.F. T.A.F.' according to whether he was (1) already registered and transferred, (2) whether his Registration is in the process of being applied for and has been sent to the Kennel Club, or (3) both his Registration and Transfer have been applied for.

THE ENTRY FORM
You will find spaces on the entry form for the dog's name, breed, date of birth, sex, breeder's name, sire's name, and dam's name. Fill these in, using the exact details given on the Registration Form. If his name

is 'Black Jack', he will be disqualified from his wins if you enter him as 'Black Jack, Sam' because you call him Sam at home. Follow the exact details of the Registration Certificate (*not* the Pedigree Form, because this may contain an error, whereupon your dog might be disqualified).

There may be a little column on the entry form saying 'Price if for sale'. You do not need to fill this in unless you want to sell the dog, and I advise you not to fill it in until you are experienced enough to realise that there are several rules and regulations attached. For example, if you do put a price, you are *bound* to sell the dog even if you change your mind. Don't fill this in unless you are definitely prepared to sell him to anyone who asks for him.

There will also be a column for the *numbers* of the classes (numbers, not names) in which you want to enter him. My advice if you have not tried him out in the ring before is to enter only two or three classes at the most.

The schedule will give you the class numbers and their meanings (definitions), as well as such details as the time, place, and date of the show, the Secretary's address and the *closing date of entries*, which you must abide by, and which is usually counted by the date of postmark. If your entry is posted too late you are likely to have it returned; enter well before closing date if possible.

Enter your dog according to his qualifications. There will be one, two, three or even four Puppy classes. These will probably be Minor Puppy (for puppies between 6 and 9 months), Puppy (for puppies between 6 and 12 months), and these two categories may also be divided into separate classes for puppy dogs and puppy bitches. You can enter for one or more of these appropriate classes. If there is a separate lot of classes for Labradors only or for A.V. Retriever (A.V. always stands for Any Variety), then enter one or two of these, preferably choosing Puppy, Maiden or Novice classes. *You do not have to enter for Open*, although the meaning given is 'for all dogs'. This does not mean that all dogs *have* to enter. It means that any dog at the show *may* enter it, if it wants to, or thinks it is good enough.

So if you have a Labrador puppy, you will probably have entered one, or perhaps two, Puppy classes, and a Labrador or A.V. Retriever or an A.V. Gun Dog Puppy, Maiden or Novice class. Leave it at that until you find out how your puppy is going to shape. There is one curious rule, which is for administration purposes: if your dog is older than 12 months (i.e. is out of puppyhood), it *must* be entered in a breed class if there is one for it (i.e. in a Labrador class, although A.V. Retriever does not count as a breed class being an Any Variety Retriever class). So an adult Labrador *must* enter in a Labrador Class if there is one, but this does *not* apply to a Labrador puppy, *unless* there is a Labrador Puppy Class.

Don't be confused if the Labrador Class is called 'Retriever, Labradors'. That is the official Kennel Club name for the breed. Or sometimes the class may be called Labrador Retriever, and again this means Labrador. The dog is a Retriever, so is called this officially. It does not mean that any Retriever can enter the class, but only Labradors. The class for all Retrievers will be called 'A.V. Retrievers', so remember your dog's official breed name is 'Retriever, Labrador'.

So, you may enter a puppy for what you like so long as it is eligible for that class, but an adult *must* enter a breed class if scheduled. Remember to note on the schedule which classes you have entered, and which dogs if you own more than one – it is so easy to forget!

People often ask whether a puppy may enter the Puppy classes on its first birthday. Yes, it may, because the *time* of birth is not known at the Kennel Club, so that it may still be under 12 months at 11.55 p.m. on its birthday. If, however, the show covers two days, the puppy's birthday would be counted as the *first* day of the show.

If when entering for the second time, your puppy has been lucky enough to win a first prize at its first show, the number of wins must be counted to see what class he is eligible for. Every first-prize win up to seven days before the day entries close must be counted, so if he wins on Saturday and the entries for the next show close on the Sunday a week away, he must count those Saturday wins, but not those on the Sunday immediately following.

However, entering for the first time should be straightforward. Fill in the details I have described, put your chosen class numbers in the appropriate column, and fill in your name and address in the space given. Make sure you sign and date the Declaration that the puppy has not suffered from or been in contact with any disease, and that it has not recently been vaccinated for distemper and hard-pad.

Enclose your entry fee, and your subscription if it is a members' show, address it to the *Secretary* (not the Treasurer or Chairman etc.), stamp it with first-class postage, and don't forget to post it *yourself* before the date and time of closing of entries.

Now you will probably hear nothing more until a very few days before the show when, if it is a Championship or Open Show, you should receive your exhibition pass. If this does not arrive before the day previous to the show, ring up the Secretary to see that your entries have arrived. Whatever happens, if you have sent your entry in time, go to the show and show in your classes. (Limited and Sanction Shows seldom send passes, to save postage.)

Provided the postmark is right when the entries do arrive you have a right to show. The local Committee may not deal with this situation. The Kennel Club will go into the matter and will decide whether you were eligible or not. For this reason experienced exhibitors *never* send cash. They send either postal orders or cheques with their entries, so that if the entries do not arrive they have some proof with the stubs of cheque or P.O. counterfoils to show they have sent it. For important Championship Shows I always get a 'Certificate of Posting' with the date clearly and readably stamped by the Post Master, so that there is no doubt that I have sent the entries in time.

PREPARATION FOR SHOW

After you have sent your entries, or even before, you must prepare your Labrador for show. This means good feeding, getting the coat in good condition, and making sure the puppy walks well on the lead. It is no use taking your puppy until you are sure of this, because the first show is quite an ordeal for it. 'It's never been on a lead until this morning', many people say to me, to excuse their puppy lying prone on the floor like a starfish when I am trying to judge its movement. That should never be the case. If you are paying good money to enter and to get there, then it is being completely wasted if the puppy does not even know how to walk up and down the ring on a lead without pulling.

Get someone to handle the puppy all over, for some days before the show, and to open its mouth to look at the teeth. The puppy will struggle madly at first at this liberty and still more when your friend handles the hind-quarters, feeling the thigh muscles and the set of hind legs, and even, in the case of a dog, feeling the testicles, as every judge has to do. So get your puppy used to all this before you start. The puppy should *not* be bathed on the day of the show, nor even for some days before. Indeed I do not like to judge recently bathed Labradors at all; it destroys the coat texture, which becomes soft and fluffy, taking several days to settle again, and may cost the puppy several places. I myself like a coat that has been brushed but *not* combed. The comb takes out the all-important undercoat, so save the comb until you are forced to use it. A good brush and polish with a cloth does not destroy the coat, but tidies it and cleans it of surface dirt and grease. Remember both when showing and judging that a Labrador may (and in my case very often will) be shooting on the high fells or in cold water the day after the show and need all the protection of weather-proofing he can get. The Labrador is a true dual-purpose dog, and no judge or exhibitor has the right to deprive a dog of this natural protection so carefully bred in by his conscientious breeder.

THE SHOW DAY

So you have now entered your dog, fed it well, brushed and polished it so that it looks its best, made sure it will walk on the lead and will allow a stranger to handle it from tip to toe (not forgetting its mouth and 'private parts'). Now the great day of the show arrives. Try to keep your Labrador out of water that morning if possible (which I have never succeeded in doing yet; at one show, my Big Gun leapt into the goldfish pond in the middle of the actual show just before she was due in the ring). I am taking it for granted that the dog is clean from skin-trouble and vermin, which is of course absolutely necessary. There is one little chore to be done on the day of the show, and that is, when giving the last brush and polish before setting off, to remove the tuft or corkscrew of hair on the very tip of the tail, which looks untidy and makes the tail seem longer than it is. Do it carefully, because the tail must taper to a point, and a tail cut abruptly straight across looks terrible. Learn to do it so that you shape the end to a point again, and leave enough hair on so that it does not look skimped or bristly with stubble. That is the only trimming you need do with a Labrador.

You will need a show-bag (the sort of shopping bag of the Marks and Spencer or Woolworth type is grand) and your equipment should consist of a proper dog-collar, a proper chain with a clip at both ends, and a lightish show-slip – usually a longish thin lead with a loop at one end and a ring at the other, so that you can make a running noose for your puppy by threading the end of the lead through the ring. This means that when showing the puppy, you can tighten the running noose to control him, while loosening it to a wide noose to show off his neck and shoulders when the judge is looking at your dog's stance.

You must bring your brush and a polishing cloth to get the coat blooming just before you enter the ring. Don't forget a safety pin, or two (in case you lose one). You will need this pin to attach your ring numbers (which you get at the show) to your lapel. A rug is useful if your dog does not chew rugs. Don't forget his water bowl, and a little bag of cooked chopped liver that you have prepared the night before, to get your dog to raise its head and look up at you when in the ring. A little jar of Vaseline is useful to be rubbed on your hands, with which you then polish the dog to get a gleam. It must be brushed well off before he goes into the ring, because you must not leave greasy substances in the coat during the actual examination by the judge.

Go to the show in very good time. You may have to 'bench' your puppy, which takes a little time, and at a small show there will be a scrum. If you go early you can find a quiet spot where you can put his rug so that he can lie quietly between classes. A show is a very stimulating and exciting event for any dog, however experienced. It will get very tired and need to rest whenever it can. It is surprising how it can take it out of a dog. I will guarantee that your puppy will sleep like the dead towards the end of the show and in the car on the way home. So keep him fresh to show off well in the ring by resting him whenever possible. Tell your children, if they are present, to leave him alone to rest between classes.

As soon as you get to the room, find a place to put his rug and get him settled. Someone should stay with him at his first show, because he will be bewildered and possibly horror-struck to see so many strange dogs and people in completely unknown surroundings.

As soon as you can, buy a catalogue and check his full details to see that there is no misprint or mistake in his name, date of birth, etc., and look in his classes to see that the Secretary (and the printer) have put him in all the correct classes and that he is, for instance, in Puppy *Dog*, and not by error in Puppy *Bitch*. If there is a mistake of any sort, go at once to the Secretary's table and get the error altered. You must do this *before* the class so that he is not afterwards disqualified by the Kennel Club, who check the winners for incorrect details and wrong entries and also for missed classes.

I like to mark the classes entered with his name in the catalogue so that while watching the show I see his name on a class two or three ahead of the one currently in the ring and so during a couple of classes can tidy him up and get him on his show-slip and well prepared.

If I am entered in a lot of classes with two or three different dogs, I write their class-numbers on their ring-number cards, upside down, so that I can read the numbers by looking down. This helps if you lose track of the show and suddenly hear a class-number called out. You can glance down at your lapel and see if the dog is in that class without recourse to your catalogue.

When your first class is called, be sure you are ready and waiting by the ring-side, with your dog all prepared on his show-slip, and with your right ring-number pinned to your lapel and your bag of small cooked liver pieces in your hand or in your pocket (a little plastic bag saves a lot of mess). When the previous class have all filed out, go into the ring with your fellow competitors. You will find that they will fall in, in a ragged line down one side of the ring in higgledy-piggledy order; don't bother to try and stand next to No. 9 if you are No. 10; you will more likely find yourself between No. 12 and No. 3. This does not matter in the slightest.

For your very first time in a show ring, don't stand modestly at what you think will be the bottom of the line. Stand in the middle of the line of 'new' dogs, i.e. dogs that have not already been seen by the judge in a previous class. The 'old' dogs will have been mustered into a secluded corner in their already decided order, but you, as a 'new' dog, will be with the unseen exhibits.

The reason I tell you to stand in the middle, not at one end, is because the judge is going to ask you to exhibit your dog and show its paces in his own particular ritual. The experienced exhibitors will know the language and if the judge says to you 'Triangle, please', you will not have an idea what he means, but they will know and will do as he asks. So by making sure you are in the middle, then whichever end of the line the judge starts at, several competitors will perform before your turn comes, and you will have breathing space to see what the ritual is and how the others do it; don't forget to watch the procedure carefully, because if you are looking at your dog or at the spectators or just day-dreaming, you won't have a clue what to do when your turn comes.

The usual ritual is this. The judge will either say 'Once round the ring,' whereupon the file will turn to their right with their dogs on their *left* sides (remember my remarks on early training on the lead in Chapter 3) and will then set off at a trot round the ring with their dogs on the side nearest to the judge. All you have to do is to follow. Three *don'ts*: (1) *Don't* tread on your neighbour's heels, for if you do, your dog will either stretch forward to smell him or, if frightened of him, hang back. Give your leader room so that you have room yourself. (2) *Don't* let your neighbour tread on your heels. If he does, turn, and say over your shoulder, perfectly politely of course, 'Could you give me a little room, please; my puppy is new to the ring?' Whereupon the person behind you will drop back a step or two. (3) *Don't* carry loose change or anything that may jangle or rattle in your pocket. You will put your own puppy off, as well as others; they hate unexplained jangling sounds.

I advise you to wear light and comfortable shoes, not only to save your feet (which will be killing you before the day is out), but also because puppies hate loud, clumping, heavy footsteps.

If the judge does not send you all once round, then he will slowly walk down the line eyeing each dog in turn from a distance (this is my method when judging). He is looking for general type, balance, good stance, and shapely lines, so as to get a general idea of what he has in the class. When you see him start down the line in this way, produce a bit of liver as he approaches and hold it in front of your dog's eyes, to get it to look up. Make sure the stance is correct, as given in the various posed photos of famous dogs that appear in this book. Don't over-stretch your dog, or let it stand all humped-up with splaying legs. Get it standing nicely with its head up looking at your hand. When the judge is two or three dogs past you, then you can relax; but if he comes back down the line still looking, see your dog is right *just before* he reaches you. I marvel, when I am judging, at the number of people who start altering their dog's stance and pulling it about just as I reach it and wish to look at it. I think this is a form of nerves, because they have the dog right just *before* you reach it and just *after* you reach it, but not *while* you are looking at it. Get it right just before the judge comes level with you, and don't fidget about while he is actually looking at the dog.

The judge will then go to the centre of the ring and will call out the dog at one end of the line (again, you are safe in the middle, whichever end he starts at). He will call the dog into a light spot and will then go over it from tip to toe (as you have already practised at home), starting at the head, looking inside the lips at the *closed* teeth (in a Labrador he will not want to see the tongue or the roof of the mouth, so the teeth must be shut properly). He will then pass his hand over every part of the dog, and will say something like 'Twice up and down' or 'Move him, please' or 'Triangle, please'. If you have watched the previous exhibitors you will by now have learned what to do and will follow their example. After you have moved the dog up and down or in a triangle exactly as the others have done, the judge will call out the next dog and you will go back to where the previous dog is standing, so that you keep in the same order of your original places.

Seize the chance *now* to let your dog relax, by sitting or lying down if he will, because the judge will continue this routine with each dog in turn and will not look at yours again until he has handled and moved every 'new' dog in the class. When the last dog goes out to the judge, there will be a rustle round the class as everyone gets their resting dogs to their feet and into position and correct stance. Now you must really try to have your dog looking its best, because the judge is actually selecting his winners. He will already know their approximate order but is trying to compute their actual placing, and is weighing dog against dog.

He may move or handle one or two again, or even go right down the line, but quite suddenly he will call certain dogs into the centre. These are his finalists. You can be delighted if you happen to be among them, but don't despair if you are left out. He will have 'finished with the rest', and out the 'discards' troop. If you are out, still have hope and go into your next classes. They will vary in strength, numbers and quality, so before the day is out you may yet get a placing; even if you don't, there is always another day. Take your luck as it comes, and look forward to the day when you and your puppy are both performing well, and get into that exciting centre position.

I shall now move on to that lovely day when you are one of the chosen few who are kept in. Even the most experienced exhibitor gets a thrill every time the judge says 'Bring in the Labrador'.

Now is the moment to keep cool and clamp down on your rising excitement. The battle is really joined, and good handling and training begin to tell. Stand exactly where the judge tells you to go, and listen to his instructions very carefully from now on, doing exactly what he says. He will line you up yet again, and will then really start to examine each dog. Next he will place the dogs in order, calling the winners into the central winning positions and marking the winning numbers down in order in his book. The steward will hand out the prize cards; if you get a prize, *remain in place* until the judge dismisses you. It is most irritating for the judge who is trying to write a quick note on his first three dogs, to see his winners snatch their prize cards and rush out of the ring waving their cards at their friends in either pride or fury. It is only good manners to stay in place until the judge dismisses you and then to murmur 'thank you' (and mean it) and move out.

What you do now depends on whether your dog is also in the next class. If he is in consecutive classes, move over to the 'old dogs' side, placing yourself in the same position as you have already been alloted by the judge, i.e. stand either above a dog if you have beaten him, or below him if he has beaten you. This makes things so much easier for the steward, whose job now is constantly to sort you into your proper places, as already decided and placed by the judge. If you can spot a dog that you *know* has beaten you or you *know* you have beaten, stand accordingly. But remember that exhibitors are often showing teams of dogs that are extremely alike, so make sure it is the actual exhibit that you have beaten, not its litter-brother.

You continue like this till your last class is finished. If by chance you are unbeaten by any dog, or have not been beaten by a puppy, and so might get the Special Award for Best Puppy, or even Best in Show, stay till the end. All unbeaten dogs will be called for to compete for Best in Show, and all unbeaten puppies, and often dogs or bitches that have been beaten only by a member of the opposite sex will be called. This last group is called because there is often an award for Best Opposite Sex. (The name of this award does not mean we are too genteel to say the word 'bitch' out loud. It means exactly what it says: 'The Best Exhibit of the Opposite Sex to the Winner of Best in Show'.)

Before you pack up and leave, look carefully at the list of Cups and Special Prizes in the catalogue to see if you qualify for any of them. For example, even if you have only won Third Prize in the A.V. Gun dog class, there may be a Cup for the Best Labrador in that class, and you may have won that. A dog has to be in the precincts of a show to win any Award. If he leaves, he can't have it.

The pattern I have described applies with only slight differences to all types of show, whether small Sanction Shows at which well-known multiple first prize winners may not compete, or bigger Limited Shows where Champions may not compete; or Open and Championship Shows (the Mecca of all exhibitors) where every dog, however famous or titled, may compete. So I will not go into it all again for each kind of show. The main differences will be that the small shows start at noon or later, while the Open and Championship Shows start sometimes as early as 9 a.m. and go on all day. At the smaller shows you are allowed to leave, within reason, when you want towards the end of the show. With the big all-day shows you will not be allowed to leave before a stated time in the late afternoon or evening, more or less whatever the circumstances, being liable to severe penalties from the Kennel Club if you do. And it is extremely important not to flout the Kennel Club. They have tremendous power over even the most experienced 'old-hand' exhibitor, and we who know are terrified of their censure because we are aware that they can make or break us if we disobey their rules.

Another difference is that at small shows you usually get your ring numbers from the Secretary's table *before* entering the ring. At big shows, the numbers will be given out actually in the ring at the beginning of the class.

Also at the big shows, and all Championship Shows, your dogs will be benched in some way, in a place of their own where they are tied up between classes and where they *must* remain all day except when in the ring or being exercised. At little shows, they can be left in the car or tied to a table leg or a radiator in the hall.

But these things vary from show to show, and can be learned quickly as soon as you have time to look round a bit. The main practice and routine will be the same, and if you read this chapter carefully before embarking on your first show you will have a good idea of what to expect.

Once you have tasted blood in the form of a card, or being 'called in' among the chosen few, you may get really and truly bitten by showing. You will find it absolutely essential to have a subscription to one of the weekly dog papers *Dog World* and *Our Dogs*. You will find you can't manage without these, because the details of all forthcoming shows appear in them; the Secretary's name and address, how to get a schedule, the dates, the closing dates, any urgent notices about the shows, such as that the entry is so big that the show is starting an hour earlier, or that it is cancelled, or the judge or venue changed. And if you do get a nice win you may find your dog's name mentioned and may even get a written critique on him by the judge, so that you know why he won or lost.

So if you are taking showing seriously, get your weekly order in and you will be kept in the picture by the dog papers.

One last piece of advice; when you get home from the show, win or lose, let the dog have a good drink. He is bound to be very thirsty; give him an extra-good easily digested meal; let him spend his pennies (remember he has had a confined day) and then let him go to bed in a nice warm comfortable bed, so that he can sleep heavily, undisturbed. He will be very tired indeed, and so will you.

7 Judging

As I said in the last chapter, once you 'taste blood' in the show ring you are apt to be bitten by the showing bug and may very well take it up seriously or as your recreation, going to lots of shows, joining all the breed clubs and travelling miles to the big Championship Shows held all over England.

With experience, you will have learned a lot about the show business, and will have begun to realise that your first dog was not absolutely perfect.

You will also know where and why your dog does not always win and will also recognise that there are 'good' Labradors and 'bad', and that these words are technical terms understood by everyone and do not refer to any sort of behaviour. Now you will be learning what makes a good Labrador, that every part of the dog is considered either correct or incorrect, and that when all these various points have been considered the dog is then considered as a whole, the results correlated and the verdict given: 'It's a good 'un,' or the reverse side of the coin, 'It's just a pet.' 'Pet' is also a technical term, meaning no good for show, and the term 'pet-quality', used by an exhibitor or judge means 'No good for showing or breeding.'

After you have been in the Labrador ring for about three years and have also exhibited at your local shows and some Championship Shows with fairly consistent success, you may be asked to judge a small match-meeting, or even a few classes of Labradors, probably at a local Agricultural Show. This is a great moment; you will feel that you have 'arrived'. So you have, and there is no reason why you should refuse the engagement, provided you have used your three years of showing to learn what constitutes a good Labrador. Up to now you have been what is called a 'ringside' judge. You will have learned a certain amount about make and shape, will know the big winners by sight, and probably their faults and virtues, with the emphasis on faults. The ringsider has a very good viewpoint from which to see the Labradors in the ring, being far enough off to see the whole line of dogs as a unit, and this is a good way to judge condition and general outline, the faults showing up much more than the virtues. From the ringside it is very easy to judge the dog that is standing out for superficial good looks and 'on his day'. That is all right for the ringsiders, who have not got the dog under their hands and are not looking under the skin to see what the dog is really made of under that superficial appearance. They will never notice that the better dog is standing quietly in line, not scintillating like a superstar, and perhaps even standing with his tail down and rather a bored expression on his face. The ringside judge will mentally give 'first' to the super-shower in super bloom; many proper judges, unfortunately, do just this all their lives and never learn how to 'look into' a dog. 'After all,' they blithely say, 'it's only a beauty competition.' With this I cannot agree. The Kennel Club requires you to place the Labradors 'in order of *merit*', not in order of beauty, and to me, in a breed that is still used for work (and indeed is the dog most frequently used for shooting in Britain), a judge who judges on superficial glamour alone is doing a lot of harm to the breed. Do not misread me here. I do not mean that the best-presented and conditioned and showiest dog should not win. What I am saying is that it should not win on that alone, but that make, shape, anatomy, suitability, and especially temperament and kindness, must all be taken into consideration as well.

So, the day you are promoted from ringside judge to judge proper, is the day to cease to judge on superficials, like a ringsider. Learn to look *into* the dogs and see how they are really made under all that bloom and presentation. After all, the day the Show Champion goes into the turnip field to 'qualify' at Trials, as he must before he can be called a 'Champion', his bloom will soon wear off to be replaced by the mildew off the turnips, and now his conformation will be what carries him to success. Many Field Trial judges hate testing 'qualifiers', considering they are wasting precious time and birds on a 'dumb blonde beauty queen', as I heard one judge call a particularly slow and ponderous dog in the field. (Another expression I have always treasured was 'A gurt good-looking good-for-nowt'; an earthier but no less accurate description.)

Although many do not realise it while they are judging, judges are actually helping to shape the breed, and unless they shape it with its work in mind, they are letting down the thousands of people, both here and abroad, who buy Labradors intending to work them and wanting the essential qualities of the breed. Most overseas buyers want their dogs to work as well as show. It is up to the judges to see that the winners have the merits of the true Labrador breed and not just a sort of glossy glamour on the day.

This business of looking right into a dog comes with practice, and your first judging engagement, even if it is only judging a four-class Exemption Show in aid of some charity, will give you more insight into the actual construction of good and bad dogs than all your ringside judging will have done.

Every judge has their own idea about what they want in a dog, especially when it comes to the finer points of a breed. From the ringside you will probably, with all your friends, have heartily condemned the Labrador with the tail sticking straight up like a flagstaff. 'Fancy putting *that* up', we all cry from the ringside, not realising that it is a super dog otherwise, far outshining the rest in head, reach of neck, big ribs, expression, coat, shape of tail. When judging only the other day, I 'spotted my winner' as a class of Labradors filed into the ring. When I came to handle it I found its mouth was really badly undershot, so undershot as to have a space between the projecting lower teeth and the upper teeth. What did I do? I tried to weigh this outstanding fault against the dog's virtues (although actually it was a small show, and the dog was not in itself outstanding apart from the fact that its competitors were rather bad). It passed through my mind that the handler must, presumably, think it such a good one as to be able to carry this glaring fault, so I looked again to see if I was underestimating it in any way. But I came to the conclusion that it was just a nice dog not good enough to carry this disadvantage. The ringside judges were baffled when they saw me pull out another for the first place, because to them it was the obvious winner. However, they could not see its teeth. I acted as I did after weighing the whole situation, the virtues and good qualities of the dog, the badness of the others and the fact that I felt the virtues did not outweigh this highly hereditary unsoundness. But how should I have acted had the dog been so completely outstanding as to be good enough to carry such a glaring fault? This is what judging is about, and the judge proper has to make and stick by his decision, while the ringsider just goes for the obvious dog. Thus there is a very big gulf between the spectator judge and the man who has to act on his judgment.

This sort of problem turns up time and time again in different guises and often accounts for a dog going up one day and down the next. With minor faults, one judge may weigh a long thin tail against flat open feet and prefer the bad-footed one to the long-tailed one. Next day another judge will consider the matter just as carefully and will prefer the one with good feet even though the tail is long. Which is right? Who can say? The tail usually denotes whether the dog will have Labrador characteristics, yet he walks on his feet. No one can tell you how to decide these things. You are now the judge and must decide yourself.

I myself think that the basic make and shape of the dog should be correct, because the construction of the frame, angles, and balance are the actual mechanism by which the whole dog functions. It is no good putting a Rolls-Royce body on an old, badly constructed, shoddy chassis, which is the equivalent of a beautifully upholstered Labrador with a badly-made anatomical frame. If you can't get a good body on a

Mrs Ruth Tenison's Ballyfrema Labradors, a splendid team of workers.

stout frame, then I myself would prefer the old body on the Rolls-Royce chassis. After all, one can renovate a body and upholstery, just as you can get a moulting coat back when the new coat comes through and can fatten or slim a dog to suit its looks, showing it only when looking marvellous. But the chassis is the thing that will crumple if badly built, so I would plump for the Rolls-Royce chassis.

People who do not work their Labradors, or who give them light work on stubbles in easy covert and on flat ground, do not always realise the terrific strain that may be put on a Labrador's frame in rough, very hilly, rocky country, with big stone walls where he will be required to make very long steep climbs and drops with a heavy bird in his mouth, as in Scotland, northern England or the Welsh mountains. Nor may they appreciate that a wildfowler's dog has to face tides, rough weather and freezing wet, that would defeat anything but a well-made dog, needing every inch of the coat and undercoat called for by the Standard.

So when starting out to be a judge, remember these working conditions and that it is conformation, not showiness, that gets the dog through the day. The bloom and sparkle and fat, prosperous body condition is for the show days only; the well-constructed, oiled and dove-tailed mechanism and craftsmanship in build and anatomy is for all the dog's life and makes his working existence easier for him. Remember that the show dog may also be wanted to work, or to breed puppies capable of doing a Labrador's job, so look deeply, not

Lawnwoods Hot
Pants of Warringah.

superficially, to find the dog of 'merit', not necessarily of 'on-the-surface' beauty.

What, then, does one want when looking into a Labrador in the ring? I can only say what I myself look for, because all judges have different ideas, and if they are experienced and really know the breed, then their judgment is as valid as mine or as any other judge's, even though we may all get slightly different results.

When I first look at my class, I am appraising the likely-looking Labradors for type and general characteristics, with pleasant expressions, shapely bodies, with good balance and symmetry. I scan the angles of forequarters and hind-quarters, whether the back is strong and fairly level, and whether the dog stands nicely balanced on his feet. One immediately spots one or two that are not true Labradors, or are over-straight in shoulder or hind angulation, have dippy backs or long weak couplings, and are obviously not in the running. I make a mental note of any dog that looks fairly likely, but make no decision whatsoever about them yet. Many give the whole class one turn round the ring, finding that this helps enormously to assess the points I have given, so as to make a start, to know how the land lies and the strength and quality (or the reverse) of the class as a whole.

When I call the dogs in one by one to run both my eye and my hands over them I judge them as follows: I see whether the ears are either too big, too long, too thin, or too small and whether they are set right, hanging close to the head and set rather far back. I feel the skull-shape

Mrs Wiley's Bell-
warde Broomsmead
Venturesome.

to see if it is clean yet broad, and not 'bossy', narrow, over-heavy or too light, whether there is growth in it, if the dog is still immature, whether the cheeks are too coarse and padded, whether the 'stop' is correct and the head like a Labrador's with no trace of Flatcoat, Hound, or Pointer. I look at the colour of the eyes, to check that they are neither too light nor too dark, but are hazel (however light the hazel) or brown. Black I personally detest, and have turned more dogs out of the reckoning for black eyes than for light. Light, I can forgive at a pinch, provided they are not glaring gooseberries, which completely spoil the expression. Black, on the other hand, give no expression at all; not everyone will agree with me here, but once again, in my view, the Standard is right, and the hazel or brown eye is the best for the Labrador's characteristic and should be judged accordingly. The muzzle I test with a thumb on each side, feeling for fullness and strength and moderate length (not shortness). A muzzle that is too short and stubby is bad for work, as is one that is too long, tapering and snipey. The muzzle is the instrument that has to carry a hare, which weighs from 7 up to 11 lb. (I once saw three hares picked at a Scottish Trial, all over 11 lb, weighed there and then at the lunch-break.) My 21-inches Labrador bitch Carry had had to pick one of these alive and kicking in very deep roots, with a long way to bring it back. I cannot imagine some of the short-faced Labradors I judge being able to do this, and so I feel once again that the Standard should be followed word for word here.

The nostrils should be wide, set at the end of a wide nosebone. This is an important point, because the surface of the nostrils only represents a little of the dog's scenting ability. The dog draws the scent in through the nostrils, which is why they must be wide, open and not pinched or button-nosed. The inside of the nose should be like a roomy chamber which can be filled with scent to allow the dog to savour and analyse it. If the chamber and lining are pinched and the nasal passages nipped, then the nose is not suitable for a shooting dog who has to work by scent alone and not sight. I like good jaws, but am not fond of over-flewed lips and chops, as these sometimes get caught up in the mouth and cause pain when the dog has to lift a heavy bird. I have seen Labradors turned hard in the mouth through over-flewing. The teeth also are important because over- or undershot mouths may affect both the lifting and carrying powers and also the digestion.

In England we do not take overmuch notice of the number of teeth, especially missing pre-molars, as long as only an odd tooth is missing. But when judging overseas this can be a most important, indeed sometimes disqualifying, fault.

Fig 5
Shoulder Angulation
A. Correct. 90° angle at shoulder. 145° at elbow. Shoulder-blade laid back
B. Wrong. Angles at shoulder and elbow almost straight. Shoulder-blade straight up
C. Wrong. Open angle at shoulder. No elbow-angle. Shoulder-blade laid back

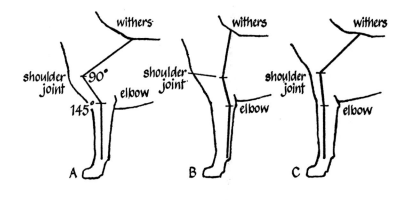

The neck should be long and strong enough to enable a Labrador to lift a bird easily. It should be clean but not so skin-tight as to appear skimped. The throat has to meet the brambles and thickets when the dog is coming through covert carrying a bird, so there should be a thickish pelt and dense coat on the throat to give protection. But nothing looks worse than a throaty Labrador with hanging flews and dewlaps. The Standard calls for a clean, strong, and powerful neck, and this describes exactly what is required.

The shoulders are a very important point, because how they are made influences the whole dog. If the shoulders are straight either at the shoulder joint or at the elbow joint, then the hind angulation must be straight too if the back is to be correctly level. If the shoulders or elbows are too straight but the hind angulation correctly sprung, the whole body has to slope towards the tail, with wrong stresses going on every joint of the back and hips and stifles, throwing the weight wrong on every part of the limbs, including the feet. So a straight shoulder and elbow means straight angulation behind if this wrong sloping force of weight on the joints is to be avoided; if all the limbs are so devoid of the correct angulation as to cause the whole weight of dog (and hare) to thump heavily on to every unsprung joint, there will be dire future results in arthritis and unsoundness.

To get the correctly angulated frame, fore and aft, is a most important thing in the dog and is the clothes-horse on which to hang a sturdy, typical Labrador. But I cannot see the use, except possibly as a fireside pet, of a beautifully typical Labrador hung on a wrong, straight-angled or unbalanced, frame. If you remember that the dog has to 'concertina' his angles at every step when working, to take the heaviness out of what he has to do, then you may see my viewpoint. But then I have trained and worked *every single* Labrador that I have ever kept in my kennel over the age of 6 months, so perhaps other show judges who do not work their dogs will not see this point. But even if they don't work their own dogs, they might at least remember that other people *do* work their dogs, and are buying from these judges' stock and winners, expecting that, because the dog is winning, it will at least be suitable for action. The Standard calls for an *active* dog quite rightly; some judges go for the heavy inactive dog actually in preference.

The body contains the heart and lungs and therefore should be strong, the chest wide enough to give room for expansion, and with good, round, deep ribs. The loin should be short, the ribs coming well back, so as not to have a cut-up Greyhound-like loin. The loin must be broad and strong, although not quite as broad as the ribs, which must 'spring', meaning that the dog should not be the same width all the way down the body. If the sides are exactly parallel all the way down the length of the dog, then the ribs are either too narrow or the dog is too fat. The ribs should spring, and the loin be very slightly waisted, although the couplings must be short. Then come the wide hind-quarters. These must be broad, wide, muscular and very strong. Skimpy, pinched hind-quarters are a very bad fault indeed. The hind-quarters actually propel the dog, the shoulders acting more as the hub of a wheel over which the dog passes at every stride, using his legs as the spokes.

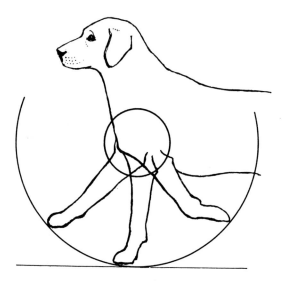

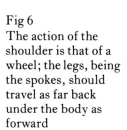

Fig 6
The action of the
shoulder is that of a
wheel; the legs, being
the spokes, should
travel as far back
under the body as
forward

The line drawing illustrates the point that the legs are nothing more than wheel-spokes, only instead of travelling on round until the dog passes over it again, in the case of an animal it is retracted, (doubled up), and comes back into position the shortest and easiest way.

So the drive comes from behind, and for this reason heavily muscled shoulders are not correct. You never see correctly-built shoulders heavily padded with muscle; they are nearly always very clean, even when the dog is in its teens.

So a clean shoulder and heavily muscled hind-quarters are correct, not the other way round.

Incidentally, weedy, thin and pinched hind-quarters on an otherwise good Labrador point towards hip dysplasia, a disease which often wastes the hind-quarters, including the leg-bones, and gives extra small hind feet.

If when judging you see thin hind legs, especially thin thighs, and hind feet definitely out of proportion with the forefeet, which appear normal, with good leg bone, then beware, and watch the hip movement very carefully. It is amazing how often one sees this wasting of thighs, leg bones and hind feet in photographs of Champions right back through history to the great Labradors of old; I am certain that a lot of those old dogs would not have passed an X-ray. The disease had not been recognised in those days, but I am quite sure a lot of them had it, just the same. They show every outward sign of the disease.

The hind-quarters should not slope down towards the tail, and the tail set should be well up, level with the dog's spine-end, making a practically unbroken line with the back level. The tail *may be carried gaily* (see the Standard). The hind-quarters must be broad and strong viewed from the rear, neither too close nor too wide, so as to give correct movement, which also should not be close or wide. There should be two distinct hams, the thigh which should be broad and muscular, and the second thigh, which must be muscular too, almost bulging until it tapers suddenly into the hock. The stifle must be sprung (i.e. bent), and the hock slightly bent too, but not sickle-hocked so that the leg comes forward under the body, and not straight so that the leg is either set too far back, or so that the dog stands straight behind with a hump over his loin and rump. Any straightness in the angle of either the stifle or hock throws not only the back line of the dog wrong, but the hips and pelvis too, and the weight does not fall correctly on to the pads of either fore or hind legs, which are affected by each other's angulation, as I have explained already.

If the angles of the hind leg are correct and the dog stands true in a proper Labrador stance, with his legs neither right under him, nor stretched right back, then the bone from hock to foot falls exactly perpendicular to the ground, at an exact right angle to the ground surface. This is correct angulation; if it does not do this, the dog is made wrongly.

To my mind a judge should *know* these things before he judges. If he then decides correct conformation is not of much importance and that the dog can manage perfectly well without it, then well and good; he may prefer, perfectly validly, to put more emphasis on other points. But he surely should *know* correct conformation before he decides to ignore it, rather than ignore it through ignorance.

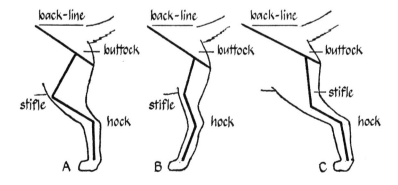

Fig 7
Hind Angulation
A. Correct
B. Wrong. Stifle straight. Sickle Hocks. Dog tends to stand on its heels with leg under body. Back often humped and hind-leg straight
C. Wrong. All angles too open, hind-leg stretched behind dog with sloping back-line

When judging, a judge 'tells' an experienced exhibitor by his actions what he is finding and what he is missing. I always look to see what the judge is discovering about my dogs. If he finds the virtues and then decides to ignore them because of the faults he also finds, that to me is fair enough. He is finding the various points I try so hard to get right on my dogs and the mistakes I have made too, and is then judging them one against the other, which is what he is there to do. It is the judge who glosses straight over one of my carefully developed good points, not even knowing it is there, that is my despair. I think bitterly: 'I might just as well have bred bad shoulders (or hocks) for this judge. He doesn't even know they exist.' These are the judges the experienced exhibitors hate privately as judges (they may be very charming people, too).

Having looked pretty deeply into the Labrador's make-up and shape, now is the time to dress the skeleton with exterior and important good points such as expression, density and texture of coat, bloom, polish, showmanship, and presentation, and having considered them singly and then as a whole, you can make your decision knowing that you have gone right over the dog both inside and outside the skin, and have correlated the facts you have found and come up with your answer. The handler will be satisfied, if he too knows his Labradors as he should, from stem to stern, and will appreciate that you have spotted both virtues and faults and given them all consideration. He will then take your decision, knowing that he has been well and truly looked at and that justice has been done.

Finally, it is the practice and tradition with Labradors to judge every dog fairly and squarely, doing your job without stinting from beginning to end. This takes some guts when you have a long day's judging, from, say, 9 a.m. to 6 p.m., as we do at Championship Shows at the present time. But it must be done, and your last class of dogs must be judged just as conscientiously as the first. This should apply to Trial judges too, but is often forgotten as the dusk draws on. To me it is unforgivable in Trials to give your last eight dogs on the first day of a 24-dog stake a hurried superficial run, and it is equally inexcusable in the show ring, even though you may be dead tired. Speed your judging up by all means – we can usually put on a spurt if we have to – but never skimp the dogs. They must be judged from first to last, even if you collapse afterwards and have to be helped from the ring. It has always been so with Labradors and must continue to be so, that every dog gets a fair crack of the whip, whether he appears first or last.

8 Breeding from your Labrador

Nowadays there is absolutely no necessity to breed from a Labrador bitch unless you really want to, because antibiotics have done away with the principal source of worry, which was that unless a bitch was bred from, she would develop a disease called metritis, which was inflammation of the womb causing an offensive discharge which ended in death unless a hysterectomy was performed immediately. So all owners of a bitch were told by their vet if consulted that they should breed from her once for her health. Modern drugs have largely done away with this danger; a bitch can now survive until her natural span of life is ended without having a litter.

However, most people who have a good pedigree bitch like to try a litter once from her, very often because their friends have booked puppies from her.

Mating

All potential Labrador breeders who have bought a bitch to found a kennel can't wait to start their first litter, so the first question is: 'At what age can I mate her for the first time?' Labrador bitches are slow maturers and are not fully developed until they are eighteen or twenty months. Up till then they are still 'furnishing', getting their strength, and even in the case of Black Labradors, still growing, although Yellows mostly mature and finish growing very much earlier. Because you do not want to stunt the full development of the young bitch, it is best to wait until at least her second season before mating her, or even her third if she is a slow grower and maturer. Any time from about eighteen months onwards is all right for a first mating, but preferably not later than two and a half years. She will be able to stand the drain on her reserves of calcium by then, provided you do not rear too many puppies on her the first time. Rearing a litter takes a lot out of a bitch, however well you feed and nurture her and the puppies.

So when she comes into season at eighteen or twenty months, you can start. Firstly you must decide on a stud dog. This takes a lot of thought, because it is best to use a dog that complements your bitch's virtues and corrects her faults, and which also connects in the best possible way in their pedigrees when combined. By now you will be following the doings of famous Labradors of the day with close interest, so will have a very good idea of which dog you want to use to her. For the first two or three times, you will be likely to choose the biggest winning dog of the day, either in Trials, if you are mostly interested in work, or at the big Championship Shows if you want to breed 'show potentials'. This is not a bad thing to do for a beginning; it is only later, when you are forming a definite strain for yourself, according to your own mature ideas, that you will start ignoring the 'titled' dogs and the big winners and will go for the dog that you feel will most suit your purpose. Many people nowadays will only use a dog if he is X-rayed clear for hip dysplasia and has his P.R.A. certificate, a good move provided they also consider the suitability of the dog to the bitch in other ways, but not if all they want is a medical chart.

You will probably have been planning on what you are going to use for months before the bitch was due in season. For those who are undecided, here are two or three important factors to keep in mind:

1. Find out from the dog owner or other expert on pedigrees whether the lines you are proposing to mate together are likely to 'nick' as we call it when two lines suit each other, with both breeders of the sire and dam having somewhat similar ideas on what they want in a Labrador.

2. Consider the colour problem. Go back and study the colour chart (page 47) and remember that while two Blacks can usually produce a few Yellows in a litter, two Yellows never produce Blacks. So if you want Blacks don't mate two Yellows together; however black their pedigree, two Yellows won't produce black puppies for you.

3. Consider the size of your bitch and whether you like her as she is, want to raise the size or lower it in the next generation, or whether you want heavier or less ponderous puppies.

4. Consider the actual faults that are there present in your bitch, and don't use a dog that also has these particular faults, or you will stamp them in.

5. Go carefully into the two pedigrees to find out, if you can, the recessive faults which lie hidden in either strain ready to pop out if you double on them.

6. *Don't use a dog if you don't like him yourself* whatever the experts say and however big the wins he has amassed. He will stamp some of his puppies with his likeness and qualities, good and bad, so if you breed from a dog you don't like, you will dislike quite a few of his puppies too, which is not the point of breeding a litter. You are trying to produce a litter of nice puppies that you yourself like, so that other people are likely to admire them too and love the one they buy. You also hope to produce, with luck, two puppies that stand out, in your opinion, so that you run them on with pleasure until you eventually

choose the one you prefer and so get a really outstanding puppy. This, after all, is the point of the exercise.

Go carefully into your choice of a stud dog and then ring up or write to the owner to book a service from him, giving the approximate time due 'in season'. Don't write, as one lady did to me, and say 'My bitch will be in season on October 12th and ready to mate,' the letter being written in April. Just tell the owner the probable month and whether you expect her early or late in the month. That is the best one can do; until a bitch actually comes 'on heat', you can't tell when she will come on or be ready; they vary so, very often from heat to heat.

I have noticed that this variation depends largely on two things. First, whether there are other bitches in the kennel; when one comes on heat she will bring on any other bitches that are within a month, or even two, of coming on. Secondly, whether there has been a cold snap in spring, or early autumn (i.e. February or October) followed by a sudden warm spell; all the bitches will then come on heat simultaneously, which is an annual curse for the stud-dog owner, who has a gap of weeks without bitches and then all the bookings clamouring to come to the dog in the same week and often on the same day. However, the stud-dog owners will cope with this to the best of their ability, and will try and fix the dates so as to stagger the actual matings. Don't worry if you hear another bitch has visited the dog a day or so before your bitch. A stud dog is in full force at these periods and can produce litters even if the matings are very close together. After all, this happens in nature and is some sort of natural provision, possibly so that the puppies in a pack of dogs are not born too far apart in time. Stud dogs in full use are often more likely to be fertile than in their first mating after a long period without bitches. I find from my records that my dogs are least fertile in July for about three weeks, so that it seems as though nature does not like September puppies. Funnily enough, one seldom gets bitches in season in July either. The chief stud periods are from early February, to April or early May, and then again from late September to early December.

When your bitch does come in season she will start to drip tiny spots of blood which, if you want to breed from her, should be carefully watched for. Hints of these are that she may lick herself a lot, or spend lots of 'pennies' very frequently in very small amounts. As soon as you see these tiny spots, get in touch with the owner of the stud dog and say exactly when you first noticed the spotting. The owner will probably advise you that the right day for mating will be 12 to 15 days after spotting was first noticed. Allowances may be made, when counting, for the owner of the bitch not being sure of the day spotting started, but from the day she starts 'showing colour', as we call it when the bitch is spotting, 12 to 16 days cover the period of 'matability'.

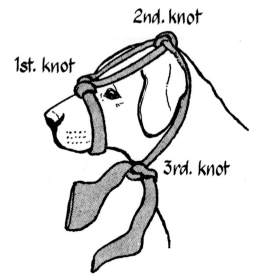

2nd. knot

1st. knot

3rd. knot

Fig 8
Stocking Muzzle. A
simple muzzle useful
when dealing with a
difficult mating, or
when giving first-aid.
Made out of a nylon
stretch stocking

Before that she will not be 'standing' – which means literally what it says, standing rigid with her tail either held right round to one side, or elevated and cocked to the side.

When she starts to pull her tail to one side when you press on the rump just forward of the tail, or if she does so when another dog or bitch sniffs at her, then she is ready to visit the dog. It is the custom for the bitch to visit the dog, he performing best on his own ground.

The stud-dog owner will know the essentials of the mating procedure. All you need to do is take the bitch, a collar and lead that can be put on tightly (a loose collar or choke-chain is worse than useless), the bitch's pedigree so that the stud-dog owner can check it again to make sure the mating is suitable (although you should already have done this), and the money for the stud fee, which is payable immediately.

The actual mating can be a shock to a new potential breeder, so I shall explain it in full.

First, there will be some preliminary play, the dog bounding and bouncing and the bitch trying to jump round at him, which must be prevented by the owner of the bitch holding her tightly by the two sides of her tight collar, so that she cannot turn on the dog. You, knowing how kind and nice your bitch is at home, will probably think this unnecessary, but the mating of two animals is more often than not fraught with unexpected difficulties, and the dog may be thoroughly put off his job if the bitch persistently growls and snaps at him, especially so if her teeth meet in him. Indeed, she may have to be muzzled, and a simple nylon stocking muzzle is shown in the drawing. Be determined; catch hold of that tight collar at each side of the neck, yourself facing forward, and hold the bitch firmly as straight and still as you can. If you suffer from a slipped disc, lumbago or any other back trouble, bring someone else with you who can do this, because the mating process takes up to forty minutes or more in entirety, and is a back-breaking job. We stud-dog owners don't earn the fee easily, I can assure you, as you are about to find out. Once you have got the bitch firmly by the head, the stud dog will come up, and will be encouraged by the handler to mount the bitch, getting up on her back immediately from behind. She, if standing properly, will switch her tail rigidly to one side out of the way. The dog will thrust several times and may then come down to take a breather before remounting the bitch. With many stud-dogs the handler can guide the dog's penis into the bitch, which is a great help, but some dogs will not allow this and will come down immediately if touched. Leave this to the owner of the dog, therefore, and concentrate on presenting the bitch to him correctly, four-square and with the head down to elevate the vulva into a position well up and out, thereby allowing easy entry by the dog. Eventually, if the bitch is ready and is a nice size for the dog, the tentative thrusting, alternating with rests for a breather, will come to an end, and mating will take place. The dog will thrust right home to his full extent and will 'tie'. This is the part that may shock or worry the beginner. I do assure you, however, that this is right and natural and (unlike other animals) is how dogs do it. Don't worry and panic; the dog knows what he is doing, though the bitch may appear distressed at first.

The stud-dog owner will ask you to hold the bitch very carefully while he or she 'turns the dog round' and the bitch may now struggle desperately and very strongly.

Provided you can hold the bitch from pulling herself free, once the 'tie' is on, contrary to general belief *neither dog nor bitch* can release themselves voluntarily, except by damaging the dog. This is why you have to hold the bitch so carefully, so that she does not gain enough purchase by wrapping herself round a tree to pull the dog loose. The tie is now firm, if properly formed, and will last from 10 to 40 minutes depending on the dog, who cannot release himself until the 'knot' subsides inside the bitch.

So now you will have a long wait, again in a rather back-breaking position, with one handler at each end. As the bitch relaxes a little, you too can relax and talk about other things, provided that both handlers remain alert enough to scotch any sudden attempt by the bitch to turn and snap at the dog, to roll over, lie down or otherwise try to get free; any of these methods on her part may result in damage to the dog. It is essential that both the dog and bitch must be kept from lying down.

The handler holding the bitch from behind must not put his or her hand underneath the bitch's tummy to hold her up, although it is the easiest way, because this may stop the free flow of semen. So, if at the fore-end, hold the bitch up by the sides of the collar or one hand on the collar and the other on the shoulder or flank, while the handler at the back end, after having turned the dog's leg right over the bitch's back so that they stand back to back, will hold the bitch upright by a knee in her flank and a hand on her thigh. The dog need not be held once he is 'turned' but, as I have said, he must be kept from lying down.

I like to have a double-headed noose-lead (not running but fixed), so that I can slip one noose over the bitch's head and the other over the dog's once they are both happy and relaxed. This means that they can now be held by this lead, allowing both handlers to ease their aching backs, knowing that the bitch is now held to the dog by this lead and therefore cannot really pull at him.

After fifteen or twenty minutes the dog will slip loose and come away. Take no notice of him; just let him off the lead when he will immediately lie down and start to lick himself clean and into place and make himself comfortable. Turn your attention to the bitch. One of you, probably the rear handler, will lift the bitch as soon as he possibly can by *both* hind legs, holding her back end right up in the air as though she were standing on her forelegs. This prevents a loss of semen if the bitch prances or turns to lick herself. Hold her up for just a few seconds, stroking her tummy gently towards the ribs so as to help the forward flow. Then let her gently down. Do not allow her to urinate; take her right back to the car, house or kennels so that she can now rest. She needs no special attention, but must be kept rather quiet and not allowed to romp about or take any walks for the rest of the day. By that I do not mean that she mustn't spend another penny that day. This would be ridiculous. It is just that we don't want to disturb the automatic flow of the semen, which can continue for some hours as the spermatozoa have a tadpole-like forward swimming movement of their own (this is why a bitch can have puppies from a mating without a tie). So leave her quiet for an hour or so before letting her spend a penny, just to be safe.

The dog will now return to his kennel and will be given a drink (very important because he will be very thirsty indeed) and any special attention, such as wiping him down with disinfectant or whatever that particular kennel-owner likes to do. One famous breeder always gives her dog a basin of milk with an egg, immediately he is back in his kennel.

The bitch goes back into the car she came in, and you now go to the house or office to pay the fee and in return receive the pedigree of the dog and, *very important*, his Registered or Stud-book number. At the time of writing, the Kennel Club also requires the owner of the stud dog to sign a form of proof of mating. The owner of the bitch keeps this, adding the name and particulars of the bitch, and completes it when the puppies are born. Without this document signed by owners of both Labradors concerned, the puppies cannot be registered. Don't forget these. You *must* have them and the correct registered name of the dog, ready for when you or your clients wish to register the resulting puppies, otherwise you will not be able to register them and they become virtually valueless, however well-bred. *All* details must be in order for the Kennel Club to accept registration. Pay your fee and take the bitch home to be kept quiet for the rest of the day (although she will want to be let out in the orchard in the normal way once she is home).

Pregnancy

You must be sure to keep her carefully confined for the remainder of her 'heat' just as though she had not been mated. Dual conception to another dog can take place at any time till she is right off heat, which may be for another week, and puppies may result from any mating. So keep her strictly safe from any dog at all, even a Dachshund. Dogs are remarkably clever at catching a bitch. I swear they borrow the step-ladder if necessary. Be really careful until about the twenty-first day, when she should be right off.

Another very important warning: it is now known that a change of diet of a pregnant bitch for the first week or ten days after mating may prevent the fertilised cells from adhering to the walls of the womb, or cause them to come away. So keep the diet *exactly* the same for the first week or so. Don't be tempted to spoil the potential mother at this stage, with special titbits, or more and richer food. You can pep up her diet with extra-good food such as first-class meat, tripe, calcium etc., later on in the pregnancy, but don't overdo it. Too rich food is worse for a Labrador than too plain. They are such good doers, and make such good use of their food, that too rich a diet can upset them completely.

Give the bitch normal exercise, lessening the activities as she becomes too heavy to enjoy exercise. Even then though she must be allowed plenty of movement about the place – free range in the garden if possible, so that she can feel fit and keep her actual weight down. Too little exercise for any mother-to-be is extremely dangerous when whelping, so she must get plenty of gentle exercise towards the end of her time. I myself let my bitches go on shooting till the fifth week when I feel it is not safe for them to be knocking about and jumping. I use my sense, but keep them to a normal but rather more gentle routine as long as I can, right up to the time of whelping.

Gestation is normally 63 days, 9 weeks to the day. Labradors vary round this average time, being very inclined to whelp a day or two early, but are very seldom more than a day late. Five days early is rather too early, and the puppies will need extra warmth and care; 3 days is pretty usual and you need not worry, but must remember, as they are a bit early, to check that they are sucking all right and that they have milk, which may not always be the case, although the milk usually does come with the puppies.

Nine weeks is exactly full term; after that one worries and wishes she could get on with it. From then on, the puppies put on about 2 oz each, every day, and the burden becomes wearisome and the puppies big. If she goes more than 2 days over, consult the vet. You will still probably be all right for another 2 days, but certainly, 3 days over is an anxiety, and I start taking mine round the lanes in the car, choosing reasonably bumpy lanes to try to get the puppies started. If this doesn't do the trick, then it is certainly a vet's job. But even then don't panic; my Ch. Midnight was 9 days overdue, and the whelping was perfectly normal.

Whelping

A week before the puppies are due, I get the whelping kennel ready. You must select a good place for your bitch to whelp, free from draughts and chill, the bed slightly raised off the floor, but not so much that if a puppy were to fall out when hanging on to the bitch's teats when she jumped out of her box, it could crawl under the bed and lie there getting chilled.

For the whelping bed, I used to advise newspaper, as did nearly every Labrador breeder. It can be renewed frequently once the whelping has taken place, and the bitch will like to tear it up when she is anxious and worried and just about to start whelping, making her bed, which releases her terrible restlessness and tension, and gives her something to do. So before she is due, start collecting newspapers and putting them aside in a clean place so that you can use them freely.

But times change and progress is made. With the invention of a new fabric, a light fleecy rug called Vetbed, a revolution in breeding methods has taken place. This rug consists of a fleecy man-made fibre which gives warmth on the top surface of the rug, while a canvas backing of a special sort allows water from the puppies to pass through on to a newspaper placed underneath the rug, with no moisture able to return. The bitch deals with any solid matter deposited on the fleecy surface, which does not penetrate the man-made stand-off fibre; the wet soaks right through so that the bed remains clean, warm and dry. We have found that this simple idea has revolutionised the rearing and well-being of the newborn litter.

Vetbeds are extremely cheap at the price, saving the loss of many puppies, but you must buy two, so that while you are washing one the second one goes under the puppies. The rug washes easily either by hand or in a washing machine, and dries quickly coming up almost as good as new time after time.

The only snag, if it can be called that, is that one is apt to rear every single puppy, thus saving some that perhaps would be better dead. For the healthy litter, it seems to do away with 'fading' puppies, one of the bugbears of breeding puppies. The Vetbed has done away with nearly all the worries of rearing a litter, and both bitch and puppies do far better than they ever did on other bedding.

The whelping box must be the length of the bitch with the length of her foreleg added in, so that she can stretch right out on her side comfortably both to whelp and also to present her full milk-bar if she wants to when the puppies are older and lying in a row to feed.

The width of the whelping box is such that when lying flat out, her feet just do not touch the side, this being the height of the bitch at the shoulder with about a couple of inches to spare. So you have a long narrowish box, length approximately 36 in., width about 26 in. I like the height of the sides to be 14–15 inches for shelter from draughts, with one of the *narrow* ends left low, as an exit, this side being only about 8 in. high. The box is made of wood, extra strong, and heavy if possible. I like a rail round the inside of the box to prevent the bitch overlaying the puppies, the base of the rail being 3½ in. from the floor of the box, the depth of rail 3 in. and the width 1½ in. This is a useful whelping bed and puppy nest in which the bitch keeps the puppies safely inside the area near the teats, between the hind and forelegs. She cannot lie away from the puppies, and they cannot get far away from her. The whelping rail will save the lives of many of the puppies, as it will prevent their getting behind her back and being laid on by her. I do stuff a little newspaper round the box under the whelping rail, so as to make it difficult for the puppies to travel round behind her whichever way she is lying, but I leave it loose and with plenty of 'give' so that the puppies sink into it if she does come down onto them heavily by mistake.

I do not myself use a covered box for puppies, unless the weather is very cold, but I make sure the air above the box is warm. Puppies do need warmth and if the weather is at all chilly I use an infra-red lamp, although I keep it well above the puppies and the bitch, because otherwise there is a danger of their being burned or dehydrated. Use a lamp with care if you think it needed; if you whelp the bitch indoors it may not be necessary. Do remember my warning in Chapter 2 not to put the box close to any solid fuel stove, whether kitchen stove or hot-water boiler, because of the heavy fumes. This is another reason why the box must be raised an inch or two off the floor. Both ground-draught and cold striking up through the floor, and fumes, are deadly to puppies.

When your bitch is about to start whelping, she will become restless, may leave a lot, if not all, of her dinner, and will generally be extremely restless and anxious and will what I call 'bang about'. Give her plenty of newspaper to tear up, which will save your curtains and furniture. (Nature tells her to break and tear up everything in sight to make a bed.) She will also pant a lot, and her face and eyes will be anxious. She will go into her box and tear up the papers, and may chew the edges of the box, which is why it should be made of hard tough wood.

She will quite alarm you with the fuss, bumping, and banging of bed-making, but will eventually go back into the bed, lie down and proceed to start whelping. She will strain, at first at quite long intervals (ten or fifteen minutes), but the straining becomes stronger and more frequent until with one push the first puppy arrives. Unless she whelps unexpectedly at night, which does quite often happen, you will have been keeping a close eye on her. So with luck you will see the first puppy arrive or if not, hear the squeaking. All puppies squeak at first, that is normal, but if the puppies mew weakly like a seagull or a kitten, then it is as well to call your vet, as the puppies may need an antibiotic injection; normal squealing and squeaking goes on for the first day, and then the puppies should settle down quietly as they get contented with the bitch's milk.

When the first puppy is pushed out of the bitch's passage, she will immediately start biting at the bag in which it is enveloped and will bite the cord in two. As some young bitches get rather frantic having puppies, I like to see she does this properly and does not either leave the puppy in the bag and the string unbitten, as though it was nothing to do with her, or overbite the bag and the cord and possibly start on the puppy too. I also like to make sure that she gets the puppy in beside her teats and starts to lick it dry. Her violent licking may upset you if you haven't seen it before, but the vigour is needed by the puppy. It gets the lungs working, and causes the puppy to squeak, thus cleaning the throat and nose of any fluid that has collected during the birth, and gets the circulation going. Once the puppy is dry and clean, it settles down between its mother's legs and close to her body so that it keeps warm. If you find she is too restless, and keeps turning round, standing up and then thumping back into the box, then move the puppies, as they are born, to a warm basket lined with cotton wool in your kitchen (out of her earshot) with a warm hot bottle, *not boiling or too hot*, which is covered with a piece of blanket. Then, when the whelping is over or when she settles a bit and starts looking for the puppies, put them back with her. This is often a very good thing to do, but normally I try and leave several if not all of the puppies with her in case she misses them and gets anxious.

She should have the puppies fairly regularly at about 10- to 30-minute intervals. About halfway through she may stop for a rest, during which time I give her some warm milk, and after say half to three-quarters of an hour she starts off again.

If she strains and strains without producing a puppy, or if the rest is unduly long, then get the vet (having warned him that she is likely to whelp well beforehand), because if induction of the puppy or manipulation by forceps is required, it should be done sooner rather than later, while the mother still has plenty of strength.

However, all usually goes smoothly with Labradors, and by the morning you should have a full litter of fat-looking puppies, already starting to suck, squeaking naturally and not mewing. The mother will be settled and lying down curled round them and turning to clean them very frequently, another natural action that is needed by the puppies, the tongue-massage causing their bowels to work. She will want to keep them absolutely spotless, so change the newspaper under the Vetbed regularly, and wash the Vetbed when you think necessary, not forgetting to use your spare Vetbed while washing the first. Otherwise the puppies may get thoroughly chilled without one, when they are already used to its warmth.

If you are an inexperienced breeder (and indeed experienced breeders often do this as a routine), get your vet to visit the bitch next morning to make sure there are no puppies or afterbirths left in her. He will give her an injection to cleanse her if necessary, and may also give her an antibiotic; he will know what is best to do, so leave it to him.

The bitch will need *very* light food for the first two or three days: bread and milk, a little chicken, eggs, fish etc., but *not* meat, as this may cause fever. She is an 'invalid' and must be treated as such. Feed her little and often. If she wants to, let her run out, just to spend her pennies, which she will wish to do well away from the puppies, and let her go straight back to them. Then leave her to sleep soundly (because she is very tired), until her next snack. Do, however, keep an ear open for a loudly squeaking puppy; it may have got away from its mother or be round behind her back.

After three days, or less if she is very well, get her gradually on to more normal food, feeding her four times a day, with milk-inducing food such as Lactol added, and with plenty of milk on her soaked bread or biscuit; go steady with the meat for the first five days.

If the bitch has done her job properly, she will have consumed the bag that the puppy is born in, and the afterbirth too, at the time of whelping (don't try and stop this, it is natural and important to the bitch). This will result in dark, foul-looking motions for the first day or two. This is perfectly in order, so don't worry. She will also discharge freely for a week or two.

Experienced breeders can help the bitch if she is in difficulties and also recognise several signs of trouble in the puppies and can deal with it, but I am not going to advise a novice to interfere with the puppies, either at birth or afterwards, because it is a complicated affair; great damage might be done and infection has to be most carefully guarded against. If in doubt, while you are still a novice *get the vet*, as soon as you suspect any sort of trouble at all.

When you get really experienced, you may often assist the bitch by helping a puppy being delivered in a normal position, i.e. head first with forelegs along the nose. The puppy may be gently drawn out by the head, but *not* if the position is abnormal in any way. I myself prefer to leave things to nature, unless I have to interfere because the bitch is tiring; because of the danger of infection, I leave well alone as far as possible. If the puppy comes rear-first, then get the vet at once, as this is an abnormal presentation and may cause problems. However, Labradors are usually such good whelpers that interference is seldom needed.

After three or four days, all should be going on well, unless the dreaded 'fading' of three- or four-day-old puppies has started. There is, so far, no known cause for this, though many suggestions have been made as to why they do it. The first sign is mewing and noisiness by one puppy, who keeps getting away from the bitch however often you put it back. As yet there is no certain prevention or cure, and work as you will, the mewing puppy usually gets weaker and colder and eventually dies. Then another will start and yet another. Luckily the entire litter seldom 'fades', just certain puppies. Apart from your vet giving the litter antibiotic injections, there is little that can be done. It is heart-breaking, and occurs in litters rather too frequently. The puppies in the litter that do not fade seem to go on as though nothing was happening. The fact that the Vetbed seems virtually to have eliminated 'fading' except in very severe cases, leads me to believe that fading is largely due to chill to the actual stomach, the least protected part of the puppy. The warm fleece has an in-built comfort, and I no longer dread fading puppies as I once did. It also seems to do away with the incidence of 'swimmers', those puppies who cannot get their legs together to crawl to the bitch. The fleece helps this, giving the swimmers a grip, so that they can keep up to the milk-bar and therefore survive. But whether this is a good thing, I cannot yet decide, as I am not sure that this fault is not carried on to the puppies' eventual puppies. Time will tell whether this saving of swimmers is a fault or a virtue.

Once the fifth day is safely past, you should have escaped 'fading', and the puppies should progress without further difficulty.

The number you rear on a bitch is your affair. I try not to rear more than five or six on a bitch at her first time of whelping, and seven or possibly eight on a bitch that has had puppies before and that I know has good, plentiful milk and can cope. But *never* more than eight, because a higher number drains the bitch, and also the puppies, of calcium; they may not get enough food, the weaker ones having a terrible struggle to get to the milk-bar at all. Many people say they are rearing huge litters successfully by either holding back the strong puppies to let the weak have first go at the milk-bar, or letting them feed in batches alternately, supplementing all puppies in turn with made-up milk. In my view, both methods are wrong. We want the strongest most viable puppies to survive; 'survival of the fittest' is a good rule. Whatever method you use, you are keeping back the strong to rear the weak, and I think this is a *bad* idea. I believe that one should only keep and breed from the strongest, best, most viable, and soundest stock.

From birth until about the 18th day, the bitch will do all that is necessary for the puppies, so you can start to enjoy them with less anxiety after the 5th day. When it comes to the 12th day the eyes will be open and the puppies will start to look at you and their mother, which is rather nice. Very soon they will be prancing round the box, and at about 18 or 19 days I like to get my puppies started with a tiny feed of 'solid' food, i.e. a small saucer of Farex made with milk with a tiny scrape of raw meat in it – just enough to colour it pink. If they enjoy this, then from there you gradually thicken the mixture, adding a few brown bread crumbs and eventually mince, until the puppies, by about 23 or 24 days, are licking the food up freely.

From now on you can go ahead with proper food, i.e. soaked puppy meal, No. 1 size, with mince, eggs, etc., added.

Four meals a day is the aim, with a snack of warm Farex last thing at night, gradually dropping to four meals in all. While feeding the puppies like this, the mother is visiting them less often, until by the time they are five weeks she only goes in at night.

See to the toe-nails and the round-worm doses, and by 7½ to 8½ weeks, the puppies will be ready to go to their new home.

Some people have great difficulty with 'getting the milk away' after weaning, and in getting the bitch's glands back up into shape, neat and tidy. The secret is to wean the puppies quickly, between 3½ and 4½ weeks. I have given the routine already in this chapter, but the mistake is often made of letting the bitch go in and give them a suck at intervals right up to 8 weeks or more, which may ruin her figure permanently.

I wean completely by the end of the 5th week, after which the bitch never goes in to the puppies again. The bitch will certainly become hard and hot with milk at first. Great care must be taken that the milk glands do not become lumpy and block up, thus causing pain, abscesses and other troubles such as milk-fever. When the bitch badly wants to go in to the puppies, instead take just enough off each teat to reduce the discomfort.

Never milk the bitch right out because this causes more milk to come. Just keep the glands relaxed, taking off as little as you dare. In a very few days the milk will recede and the glands start to return to a normal size. It is essential to watch the glands very carefully at least twice a day until the milk has gone back, feeling the whole length of both sides (do not forget the very back teats). If lumps are felt, then milk must immediately be removed and the lumps gently massaged to unblock the glands and keep the milk moving towards the teats.

Every care must be taken over this, or serious trouble can ensue.

An inexperienced breeder may be very worried if the brood bitch starts to vomit her food for the puppies during weaning. The new breeder may be disgusted, fearing that the bitch is ill, abnormal or vicious. Very often he calls in a vet.

I do assure novice breeders that this is nothing disgusting or abnormal, but is a marvellous natural instinct, which bridges the gap in the wild between milk and solid food. The bitch mixes her own dinner with her saliva and digestive juices, also partially masticating it and then deposits it for the puppies, which can then digest it themselves.

Although absolutely natural and the sign of a very good, devoted mother, this practice does pull the bitch herself down very much – hence the extreme thinness and ragged appearance of the she-wolf or Cape hunting-dog in the wild.

With the help of a good breeder, no bitch need suffer this hardship although it is a very difficult practice to prevent.

Whilst the puppies are being weaned, you may find that when the bitch approaches them they will lick her mouth and her face to induce her to vomit. This is a signal to her, and she will immediately oblige them; they eat her dinner, or part of it. She usually retains a little, so that she does not actually starve. She will get so used to this practice that she will even go to the door of her kennel, or if possible, that of the puppies, and deposit the food as near as she can get to them. If the puppies cannot get to it, she will eventually re-eat it herself. Don't blame her for this. It is her natural instinct, and after two or three days she will cease to vomit, when she finds the puppies are not taking it. The answer, then to this behaviour, is to keep her shut right away from the puppies until she forgets about it, or knows that the puppies are somehow managing without their extra supplement.

Don't feel worried if she vomits, but take steps to keep her shut away at dinner-time during the necessary week or so when she wants to do it. Both she and the puppies will thrive without having to use this ancient instinct.

9 Ailments and Disease

Labradors, owing to their conformation and thick dense coat and pelt, suffer far less from minor ailments than most other breeds. They have come from a hard school, the coasts of Newfoundland, and have had to fend largely for themselves (the survival of the fittest), so have become able to withstand major hardships, such as sharp edges of broken ice (which seem to have no power to cut a Labrador's legs) and bumps, falls and broken limbs.

In spite of this, accidents occasionally do happen which must be dealt with. My strong advice throughout this chapter is, 'If in doubt get the vet'. So every word you read in this chapter is punctuated with that advice and I mean it. Vets are very busy people and hate having their time wasted, but I can tell you with great conviction that any vet worth his salt would rather be called too soon than to find the dog so ill as to have to go all out night and day to save it. So to punch the idea strongly home, I repeat, 'If in doubt, get the vet'.

Very minor ailments you will be able to cope with yourself, with the aid of a small medicine chest. Mine contains:

Bottle of Dettol disinfectant and of Jeyes Fluid (both clearly labelled).
Thermometer (an absolute necessity in my opinion).
Several cotton bandages of different width.
Roll of lint and roll of cotton wool.
Roll of adhesive tape. Box of small adhesive dressings.
Pair of scissors. Pair of tweezers.
Baby's feeding bottle with tiny teats.
Good insecticide powder, to eradicate fleas and lice.
Screw-top jar of canker powder (recipe to follow).
Several jars of a skin-dressing called Bob Grass, obtainable from the maker, or at some pet shops, but difficult to get.
Bottle of the pink medicine given by chemists for babies' tummy upsets, which contains kaolin (known in our family as liquid cement).
Bottle of Milk of Magnesia, to be used either as a medicine or as a skin dressing in cases of overheated eruptions of the skin.
Tin of Vetzyme tablets, as a tonic.
Packets of round-worm tablets, either Shirley's or Bob Martin's.
Two packets of tape-worm tablets.
Bottle of Friars Balsam. Eye ointment (from your vet).
Tin of Antiseptic Powder for drying up wounds.

This completes all the necessities for ordinary first-aid. Other medicines as ordered by the vet should be obtained either from him or on his prescription from a chemist, none of the above needing a prescription, and can be bought over the chemist's counter (except Bob Grass, which may have to be ordered from a pet shop).

Cuts and scratches

Ordinary cuts and scratches, if very slight, I leave completely alone, not even disinfecting. They seem to heal best if the dog licks them. With rather more severe cuts (which are indeed rare, many Labradors never having one in their whole lifetime even if hard at work over barbed wire etc.), I pull the edges together, again not disinfecting unless there is some known pollution or danger, and hold with adhesive tape or a small dressing, whichever is suitable, but always finishing with the roll of adhesive tape as the dog finds this difficult to get off. I keep the dressing on as short a time as I can, just till the edges have tightly congealed together, whereupon the dog will complete the cure with its tongue.

For really bad cuts, I put lint, cotton wool and adhesive or bandage (depending on the whereabouts of the cut), and get to the vet for stitching if necessary.

Bruises

Bruises recover spontaneously, provided no bone is cracked underneath, but badly bruised ribs should go to the vet in case of a cracked rib, which may happen, although a Labrador is so strong and elastic-ribbed that it takes something like falling over a cliff or being swept down on a flood on to a rock to crack a Labrador's ribs. Cracked or broken ribs require a vet's attention.

Skin trouble

For skin trouble, I first squeeze the anal gland under the tail, the cause of a lot of wet eczema especially round the base of the tail. This is a dirty job, but one you can do yourself once you have the hang of it, although you must be shown how to do it first. Every dog should have its anal gland watched – although few owners even know it exists (poor dogs). Once the anal gland is squeezed (incidently the *healthy* discharge is a dirty deep reddish-brown, the unhealthy being pale green or greenish yellow) the wet eczema patch must be dealt with. I dry it up with the antiseptic powder and when it is dry, probably after a day, I apply the Bob Grass ointment to regrow the hair. The patch *must* be really dry and have turned grey, like an elephant's skin, before treatment with ointment. If it is still red and oozing, keep on with the powder for another day or two, then dress with Bob Grass. The grey patch takes a long time to grow hair, but will do so, however unlikely it looks, recovering completely with time and Bob Grass.

Eyes and Ears

Sore eyes I treat with eye ointment given me by the vet. Don't experiment here. Eyes can be very delicate. For ears, I dress every dog about every two months with the canker powder we have used for years, this being the recipe: 4 parts boracic powder: 2 parts zinc oxide: 1 part iodiform. Place a little heap on the blade of a pen-knife, and, pulling the ear cavity towards you until you can see clear down the ear-hole and have a straight open passage to the depth of the ear, carefully drop the powder down. Close the flap of the ear and massage *very gently* (important) to spread the powder as much as possible. Hold the flap closed for quite a time before starting on the other ear; the fumes of the iodiform work to kill the canker mite, which is a living organism. This is a preventative more than a cure, although it will put mild cases right. If the ear is at all bad, or very dirty inside with a reddish brown deposit, go to your vet. *Do not* mess about yourself with cotton wool on orange sticks: the ear is delicate and should not be messed about with by amateurs. Incidentally the dogs actually come to like the ears being dressed with the canker powder.

Mange and parasites

If your dog gets very itchy all over and is restless, scratching constantly and rather fusty-smelling, go to the vet. It may have some rather difficult disease like mange, although it won't develop mange spontaneously because it, like canker, is caused by a living organism and is picked up from another mangy animal or from dirty bedding.

Many different mites and vermin may be picked up on straw, so if the skin is really troublesome get your vet to diagnose the trouble properly. To keep a dog in good health feed a balanced diet and don't touch or pat dogs with skin-trouble yourself, as mange can be transmitted by hand. Use your flea and louse powder regularly, especially in summer, and also in summer boil nettles in the broth saucepan, and add both broth and leaves to the dinner.

For the prevention and control of worms, I have already advised on worming young puppies for round-worms, but in addition I boil apple skins and cores (and indeed whole apples) in the broth occasionally, and also very occasionally an onion or two. These are both wonderful for worms, but should be given as a 'shock' dose, not every day or the worms become adapted to resist them. Regular tape-worm doses should also be given about twice a year, or more often if on sheep or rabbit ground.

Accidents
In accidents, broken bones may occur, but very rarely in Labradors, whose bones are extremely strong and well protected by muscle and thick skin. Bind the part pretty tightly with bandages to act as a sort of splint and carry the dog; two people are necessary for this, one to hold the dog very still if you go by car. Get to the vet as quickly as possible.

In the case of a cut which bleeds really excessively, especially if spurting blood, put a cotton bandage *above* the cut and apply a tourniquet by turning a pencil or toothbrush handle tightly inside the bandage and tying or holding firmly into place, at least to lessen the flow and to stop it if possible. It is as well to learn the possible pressure-points as this may come in useful in an emergency, but even if you don't know the pressure points, use your common sense and apply the aforesaid tourniquet. Don't forget to release it for a few seconds every 15 minutes. This *must* be done, even if bleeding immediately starts again, because blood must reach the pressurised cells every so often or they die. Get to *any* vet or doctor as soon as possible and apologise afterwards if you haven't been able to go to your own vet. The great thing is to get the bleeding stopped professionally. It doesn't matter who does it so long as it is done quickly, before the dog bleeds to death.

Broken tail
'Broken' tail in a dog is quite common, the tail hanging limply from about one-third of the way down. This looks terrible, but is actually very mild. It means one of three things, either the dog has had the first swim of the season the day before, possibly in chilly water, though the swim alone will do it; or he is sleeping in a draught and has got a chill; or he has been dead tired possibly with his first day's shooting or an extra hard day the day before.

In all these cases the dog will be better in probably one or two days, three at the most. This condition of 'broken' tail is so common to the breed that all Labrador breeders and judges recognise it and we show our Labradors in spite of it. It is only stiffness, and gets better without treatment, so don't worry at all. For any mild stiffness, say after shooting, a warm bed out of draughts is the answer.

Feet
For sore feet or for the pink lumps or swelling (interdigital cysts) that sometimes appear between the toes, dip the foot in friars' balsam. This may sting the dog at first, but soon seals the surface of the sore and helps enormously to take the pain out. The dog won't like it at first, but usually doesn't really mind too much, making a slight fuss but settling down with the foot in it quite happily. It's the idea he doesn't like more than the actual treatment. I do this for a day or two and

seldom have foot-trouble, either from sore pads or interdigital cysts. They usually soon disappear with the friars' balsam, but if they should persist or if the sore foot is very bad, then it's a job for the vet. After dipping the foot, hold it in the air to dry before letting the dog get down on to it. You find it makes a hard sort of skin, also hardens and withers the actual skin of the pad itself, making a protective skin. Don't get too much on to the actual fur of the leg or foot, because it dries hard and spiky and can be uncomfortable and bad to get out; also, being slightly sticky, it attracts dirt, sticking the hairs together like a sergeant-major's moustache. Interdigital cysts usually mean the dog is slightly run down; some Vetzyme tablets help. The floor of the kennel should also be washed down with a weak solution of Jeyes Fluid.

Distemper

Distemper, hardpad and the related diseases are a great danger. If your dog wakes with green matter in the eyes, take the temperature immediately. A puppy's normal temperature is 38.6°C(101.5°F), rising if excited, or sometimes towards evening, to 39.2°C(102.5°F). Anything over this is a sign of danger. The vet must be called immediately, and the puppy isolated and kept very warm and quiet. If you are unlucky and have contracted one of these allied diseases in your kennel, then from now on it is the vet's job, and good nursing is necessary. Follow the vet's instructions to the letter, and keep the dog warm and quiet in a darkened room. When the puppy is convalescing, you will be well advised to treat it as a convalescing invalid for much longer than you want to, because relapses are very dangerous, and the Labrador is still extremely weak and vulnerable. Your vet will tell you this, and I reiterate it. The puppy will need very careful feeding to build up its strength, with such invalid light delicacies as chicken, Brand's Essence, fish, rabbit, etc., to encourage it to eat. The big tin of Vetzyme tablets is also a great help giving yeast and the vitamin B complex. It is a long slow job building up the puppy after distemper, but is well worth every bit of trouble, provided the puppy is fully recovered, without nervous symptoms such as chorea (or St Vitus dance as it was once called) in which case you must work out for yourself whether the puppy should be kept alive or not. This can only be your decision, but don't let sentimentality and the fact that the puppy has fought gamely for its life (and you have, too) outweigh your common sense. The puppy has to live for another eight years or more, and if it is left with a really bad disability, think of it and not of yourself and your own feelings.

Kennel cough

There is a nasty disease called kennel cough, which does not appear to be related to distemper, but I believe is allied to Asian 'flu and

Newmarket cough in horses. This is a troublesome little husky, light cough high in the throat, and although it appears to be nothing much it should be nursed very carefully, the dog kept warm and dry, and the vet called. So far there is no quick cure, but the vet will give injections that help, especially against secondary symptoms. Kennel cough is a slow job, and will run right through the kennel regardless of distemper injections, etc., or whether the dogs have had it before. Any strong dog in good fettle appears to make little of it, but any that are in any way weak or pulled down (e.g. puppies, mothers recovering from the effects of a recent litter, dogs with slight heart or kidney trouble etc.) find it very difficult to throw off, and indeed may die of it. So treat it as dangerous, just as you would distemper, especially during convalescence. It is a strange disease with practically no symptoms except the husk in the throat, a pearly white teardrop in the corners of the eyes, and the whites above the eye are very faintly flushed with pale shell-pink instead of clear white (in distemper they are an angry red). Because of this lack of symptoms, people treat the disease as a mere nothing, often with disastrous effects, even taking the dogs to shows, and thus infecting hundreds of other dogs. They should be treated and isolated just as carefully as in distemper or hardpad and convalesced just as carefully too.

Colds
Dogs can and do catch common colds, which may give alarm for a couple of days but clear up without trouble. Not all dogs are subject to them, but I have had several that caught them very easily, no harm resulting.

Stomach upsets
Tummy upsets are a nuisance, and always worrying because they may be symptoms of something more dangerous. I always rush to the thermometer, and if the temperature is up, call the vet. If there is no temperature, then I *tighten* the diet (not putting the dog on to slops or milk which give loose tummies) and feed stiff rice puddings until it clears up, which should be the next morning. If the stools continue loose, or if there is any blood, call the vet.

That concludes the minor ailments that affect Labradors; the serious distemper illnesses or kennel cough are jobs for the vet and he will give you instructions. With these diseases, it is essential to get the vet to the dog as quickly as possible, before they take a real hold. Time is of the essence, and the vet will thank you for speedy action.

Breed Problems

Now we come to the three main bugbears to the health of Labradors, the three hereditary diseases: hip dysplasia, progressive retinal atrophy (a progressive form of blindness, hereafter called P.R.A., which is how it is generally referred to), and entropion (ingrowing or in-turning eyelids and lashes). The incidence of P.R.A. and entropion is very rare in the breed nowadays. Hip dysplasia is unfortunately all too common.

If you are going to breed Labradors, you will very soon be aware of these diseases, but whatever you do don't let them get you down. Every strain can suffer from any of these at any time even if 'clear' up to date, because of the introduction of the genes from any mating.

These diseases are certainly in the breed, although P.R.A. and entropion seem to follow only certain lines and/or recipes and matings. Hip dysplasia (or H.D. as it is referred to) is, I believe, in every strain of Labrador, is part of the breed, and I'm sure has been present ever since the Labrador was first described in Newfoundland in the early 1820s. (A contemporary remarked on the weakness of the hind-quarters and noticed that the dogs could swim and run well, in spite of this weakness.) So H.D. will be very difficult indeed, in fact almost impossible, to eradicate in my opinion, being part and parcel of the breed.

Progressive retinal atrophy
P.R.A. is the easiest of the three to eradicate, and should under the present method of procedure be wiped out in a very few years. Dr Keith C. Barnett M.A., Ph.D., B.Sc., M.R.C.V.S., of Cambridge, is to me one of the great heroes of Labradors, having taken the lead and done the research. He himself has 'vetted' the eyes of thousands of Labradors all over the world, either passing them or failing them with complete accuracy, and also training other vets to do the same. Practically every reputable breeder has every dog they own examined for P.R.A. Labrador breeders have complete trust in Dr Barnett, and I have never heard of him making a wrong diagnosis. We are rapidly stamping out this disease, to my mind entirely through his skill and devotion. He is indeed a great man and a saviour of the Labrador breed. We cannot be too grateful to him. This clearing of P.R.A. is the greatest step in the right direction that we have ever had in Labradors.

Entropion
Entropion is a more difficult thing to pin down. If you have certain bloodlines in your pedigree, it will crop up at intervals, but not being a

simple recessive, we find the recipe that produces it difficult to describe with certainty.

If your dog is unlucky enough to develop entropion, it is a specialist vet's job, and either means an operation on the lids if bad, or the injection of a roll of oil along the rims of the eyes if slight. Sometimes, instead of the oil injection, the lid is slightly burned or cauterised which causes a scar to pull the eyelid back (as does the oil); this may be all that is required. The remedy is simple in the hands of a good vet and causes little and only temporary discomfort to the dog. But the condition is hereditary, which must be remembered when breeding plans are being made. The choice of bloodlines to avoid entropion must be most carefully gone into, and the greatest care in choice of mate taken.

Not being a simple recessive, but having a complex inheritance, entropion can be bred completely out of the strain in one generation if the right bloodlines are used.

Hip dysplasia

Now we come to hip dysplasia, which is the bugbear you will certainly meet if you are breeding Labradors seriously. A tremendous lot of work both in research and on the part of Labrador breeders has gone into this annoying disease. Many kennels have X-rayed their stock for several generations; we have all scrapped good dogs because of unsoundness, and the utmost effort has been put into the eradication of H.D. But alas, we still know next to nothing about it and its pattern of inheritance, so we are still acting in the dark.

There are three choices open to you. The first is to take no notice whatever of the disease, just scrapping or giving away obviously unsound puppies and breeding from the others without even knowing how they stand from the X-ray point of view. The second method is an extension of the first, and is the one I have followed ever since I first panicked when H.D. was described, and like everyone else, went mad, scrapping everything, X-raying everything and generally becoming obsessed to the extent that I could think and talk of nothing else on the subject of Labradors. I found I was scrapping all my good dogs and keeping bad, so at last saw sense and changed my tune. My method now, and that of a good many breeders, is to look constantly at my puppies, my older stock, and my choice of mates for my bitches, also watching the various stud dogs' progeny in the ring and in the field. I then try to breed only from the ones that satisfy my eye, taking the risk of an occasional error and an occasional lame puppy. I do not X-ray all my stock, but take a three- or four-yearly spot-check on my current batch of yearlings to see how I am faring. By this method I have lessened the incidence of H.D. in my stock, which seems to prove my method is working pretty well, although I still get an occasional H.D. puppy cropping up.

This method means that I keep the dogs I like, and breed very carefully from them, scrapping the visibly wrong puppies. This, after all, is the time-honoured method by which all British livestock has been bred through the years.

The third method is used by many breeders. This method involves X-raying every dog and bitch in the kennel and keeping those with a very low hip-score. This on paper is by far the best and most ethical method, and I used it myself at one time, until I found my stock was deteriorating generally, instead of improving, so changed to the second method.

Those breeders who put H.D. first and foremost scrap a lot of lovely and useful stock and are forced to breed from less good.

Unfortunately we do not yet know how or why H.D. crops up, although we know it to be basically hereditary, often being 'triggered off' by outside factors such as the puppy being too fat too young, or having too much violent exercise, or too little. I am certain too that certain brands of distemper injections trigger it off in my own strain and I avoid these like the plague.

People dread H.D., thinking that any dog that has it is in constant pain and disability. This is not so, and in nearly every case except the very bad, there is little sign of the disease; it causes no discomfort as a general rule. Indeed the Field Trial dogs often have it without anyone realising until they are X-rayed. It usually doesn't make any difference at all to their fast work, jumping, or swimming.

These factors all make it a difficult disease to know how to deal with it. I have laid out the methods and must leave you to choose your own.

I am pretty sure that you will start with method three, 'total X-ray', and eventually go to method two, trying to keep clear by eye, and X-raying occasionally to see how you are doing. The local gamekeepers, who cannot afford to X-ray and wouldn't bother anyway, because so long as a dog can do the required work, that is good enough for them, will continue on method one, as they always have done. And my final word on the subject of H.D. is this: I am sure that given our present knowledge of the disease, the users of all three methods will end up with exactly the same incidence of H.D. in their kennels: a few clear dogs, a few doubtful dogs (if X-rayed to find out) and the odd 'H.D.-crippled Labrador', just as we have now.

The new and dreadful disease of Parvo Virus which first struck in 1978 or thereabouts is still being researched, especially at Glasgow.

Preventative injections are given in puppyhood, but as not much is yet known about this scourge and advice changes almost monthly I cannot give you much help. It is the worst of illnesses and advice about your new puppy must be sought from your Vet at the earliest opportunity. He will give you the latest advice from the Veterinary Colleges which are carrying out the research.

10 Training, Shooting and Field Trials

Once the teeth are right through the gums, so that there is no fear of the puppy having a sore mouth or loose teeth, real training may begin. This means any time after 5½ months (see page 43).

The puppy should of course already obey the command to 'Sit' and 'Stay' which I have gone into in Chapter 3. He will also have learned to walk on the lead without pulling, if my advice has been followed, so that his early steps towards gun training have already begun.

Once he knows these three simple and basic lessons, which all Labradors should be taught whether they are going to be shooting dogs or not, he is ready to go straight ahead with the first proper lesson, and from now on, as soon as he sees the training equipment in your hand he must treat his lessons seriously and in a professional manner, although he is still so young.

From the moment you open the kennel door, he is now 'under starter's orders', and must not be allowed to play or fool about. He will very soon realise that, and any orders must be obeyed immediately and properly.

The equipment needed to train a puppy is a strong-sounding, good old-fashioned pea-whistle. Don't bother with silent or horn whistles, or with a row of pan-pipes, which some trainers (mostly amateur) have hung about them like a one-man-band. All the necessary orders can be given on one whistle, and when needed it must be audible above the tremendous noise the dog himself makes as he gallops and jumps through the rattling turnip and kale leaves.

Buy a loud shrill whistle to make sure the dog hears it, then use it as little as you possibly can. I have found over the years, training, Trialling, and shooting, that the less the gimmicks and clutter, the better. One whistle is better than two to fiddle about with with cold wet hands, and has exactly the same effect. The sole purpose of a whistle is that it should be heard.

Two or three dummies will be needed. A stuffed wool sock makes a good dummy – stuffed with straw, newspaper or nylon stockings, or anything small, soft, and safe. For more advanced lessons, a bigger set of dummies will be needed, and I use either stuffed socks made very firmly with no loose ends, or a few professionally-made canvas dummies which float in water. For my own use I cover these with a wool sock or a rabbit skin, so that they are not hard and slippery to the dog's mouth, which may sow the seeds of a hard grip and consequent hard mouth, all too prevalent in Labradors, who tend to have a quick, snatching 'pick-up' unless every precaution is taken.

My dummies all have wide strong elastic bands a few inches from each end, so that as the dog progresses a pheasant wing, duck wing or even woodcock wing can be attached firmly to the dummy and be held in place at each end. The great thing with any dummy, from the very first, is that it should have no loose ends for the puppy to pull out and play with, for this starts the bad trick of worrying and shaking a dummy, which is hard to stop once started.

I usually have three or four dummies handy about the place, one at least being a floating dummy, and more if I can get hold of them.

You will need two or three cords of slightly different lengths, some the length of an ordinary lead when completed, one or two rather longer for when you want to let the dog have a bit of licence yet still have him on the lead. You will also require a long check-cord, so that you can send him out for a thrown retrieve and prevent him going off with it to the bushes, or can tow him towards you if he starts playing with and mouthing the dummy instead of fetching it. It is also useful if

'Big oaks from little acorns grow.' Mrs Gwilt's Sunnybrae Drumkilbo being schooled over an improvised training jump (*right*); training leads on to (*left*) performances like Major Bruce Kinloch's Ridley Logie clearing a huge 'double' post and rails.

he starts walking round and round you instead of delivering the dummy right up to hand.

To make these cords, buy a length of thinnish washing line (the cord type, or nylon, although this latter tends to be slippery). Make a fixed noose to fit your hand comfortably at one end and a running noose for the dog's neck at the other. This may be done either by attaching a strong metal ring at this end, so that you can form a noose by threading the handle-end through it, or with a knot, made so that the cord runs easily through it. It doesn't really matter how you do it so long as you end up with a cord–lead, with a handle at one end and a running noose at the other.

I like to make the lead long enough to be able to put some knots in the *handle* end, so that I can put my foot on this end instead of holding it, the knots ensuring it does not slip from under my foot if the dog gives a sudden violent jerk. I also put a stop-knot to prevent the noose from tightening and choking the puppy if it pulls the noose tight.

So to sum up on your equipment, three items are needed for the start of training: a loud pea-whistle, two or three suitable dummies, and two or three cord–leads of different lengths.

A good book on training is a great help and I recommend *Gundogs, Training and Field Trials* by P. R. A. Moxon (Popular Dogs).

Choose a nice day to start the puppy, when it is obviously feeling in good form (indeed you must both be feeling perfectly fit), so that no lack of mental or physical strength interferes with the training.

Training with a dummy
Select a quiet place, and a time when you will not be disturbed or the puppy's concentration broken. See that the smallest dummy you have got has no loose ends (important), stand with your back to his kennel direction, and then tell the puppy to sit at your left side on his cord. All training, from the very beginning when the puppy is first taught to sit and to walk on a lead, takes place on the *left* side, because that is the side away from the gun, which is usually carried on the right arm.

When the puppy is sitting and looking up at you, wave the dummy at him temptingly, holding the cord, then throw the dummy into the open so that he sees it and as it goes he rushes to get it. Drop the cord as he goes, so that he has a free run for it. As soon as he reaches it he will usually snatch it up without thinking. As he does this, turn and run away yourself very quickly indeed, calling him and clapping your hands. He will look up with the dummy in his mouth and will rush after him. He will probably try to dodge round you to get to his kennel but you must be ready for that and intercept him, getting the dummy from him if he dashes past you, easing it gently out of his mouth with your fingers *behind* the dummy in his mouth, encouraging him to open

Ridley Logie shows evidence of an exceptionally tender mouth on a woodcock, a retrieve that many Labradors detest.

it. Then give him lots of patting and encouragement so that he knows he has done something clever, although he won't be able to think what. Pick up the lead and walk him about at heel for a minute or two, then repeat the performance *once more only*. Once this lesson has been performed successfully, the big hurdle has been jumped and he is started. Take him back to his kennel, still walking to heel on the lead, and put him away to think about the lesson. By 'put him away', I mean exactly that because, as I have said, lessons are lessons and must never be confused with play or free time.

Leave him free from training for the next two days, to grasp the idea. Dogs definitely think about their lessons while in the kennel, whether consciously or sub-consciously. They need time for the lesson to sink in.

Once the puppy has picked up the dummy a couple of times, he must never again be allowed to go right in and pick it up without orders. Restrain him gently with your hand at his second lesson, and after only a few seconds, say 'Hie lost' with a very strong forward urge in the direction yourself, pointing at the dummy and urging him on. Later, have the cord under your foot when you throw, so as to check him if he does go, when you make him sit and wait a moment before again giving him the 'hie lost' signal.

After a few lessons like this, he will be ready to be made to 'Stay' while you move forward to throw the dummy. He should still be on a longish cord, so as to prevent that 'run in' without orders to go. But very soon you will have him sitting and waiting till you tell him to go.

Now vary the lessons. Throw a dummy a few yards to the side as well as the retrieve dummy ahead, and stop him from going for the one you have dropped to the side, saying 'No' very firmly and sending him on to the other. Once this is grasped, then the way is open to you for endless variations of the theme. You can throw a dummy to each side and send for the one you want and then the other; or one behind and one in front, and so on *ad lib*. The only thing is that the puppy must never be allowed to run in, or to get the wrong one, and if this happens 'No' must be said firmly and the dummies replaced, the puppy made to wait and then to fetch the correct one. In other words, *never* let the puppy get away with anything without putting it right, and this principle applies all its life.

Once the lessons of the 'double' retrieve are learnt (i.e. with the dummy and the diversion dummy, which may be picked by the dog or by hand as you please), then he must learn the same lesson in water. There is usually very little difficulty in introducing a Labrador to water, provided the coat is good and thick, as it should be. I like to let my puppies play in the water and get them used to splashing about. In summer or late spring, I take the Labrador to the water's edge, sit him on the shore a little way back and then throw the floating dummy just in his depth. He is sent for it, rushes in, and by stretching his neck just gets the dummy. *Immediately turn and run away yourself.* This is important because you want to prevent him from stopping and dropping the dummy while he shakes. So try and keep his forward impetus going with your own backward impetus. It is fatal at any stage of a dog's training to stand like a stuffed dummy yourself. Use every means in your power to get the required result performed as speedily as possible. Throw yourself into it body and soul. There is a saying in hunting: 'Throw yourself over the fence and the horse will follow,' and that explains exactly what I mean. Use *yourself* to get the dog to do it.

Make up your mind to get that puppy out into the water and back with the dummy right to you on the bank without putting it down to shake itself, and if you act fast and definitely enough it will follow.

Next time, throw the dummy just out of reach of the puppy and it will try to get it, stretch to its full extent and probably just topple forward and have to become waterborne to get it. Once it has done this, the main battle is won and it will soon learn to swim freely and get the dummy at any distance. Almost any true Labrador gets to adore water work and enjoy the more difficult exercises such as diversion-dummies on water, taking hand signals, and crossing water to hunt the other bank.

The correct entry for a Labrador is to slide in without overmuch splashing and swim quietly but quickly ahead, low in the water, making as little disturbance as possible apart from the wake. After he has become adept at this, then you can teach him to jump in off a landing stage, high bank or boat, all very useful when wanted. In these cases a dog must jump in, and a bold water dog will do it and enjoy it, and all credit to him, but let him keep this method of entry until it is needed, entering fairly quietly and smoothly at other times.

I hate a dog with a boisterous noisy entry into water. Dogs should enter quietly like otters, thus not disturbing unshot duck on the water or downstream, who will feel the shock waves of a noisy entry and will clear off immediately. Also the noisy splashy dog is apt to sink his bird or even send it floating away on the shock wave of his bad entry.

Now that the dog is well on with his dummy training, able to be directed on to whichever of two or three dummies you want, in covert, the open, or across water, and is familiar with other variations and refinements on land or water, he must now get accustomed to gunfire. Introduction to the gun must be done carefully, as many puppies are sensitive to loud noises at first. Some puppies, of course, never mind at all, not even flinching at the first shot they ever hear, but there are two other kinds of puppies, the first being the most usual, that is gun-nervous puppies, and the second truly gun-shy puppies. Take no chances, but start off as though the puppy is gun-nervous, to be on the safe side. Get someone sensible to help you, and use either a .410 gun, if possible with short cartridges, or a cap-pistol, such as a starting pistol.

Send the helper well away downwind, warning him to fire up and away from the puppy. Make sure you are somewhere where there will be no echo, because that may frighten a puppy. Sit the puppy down and chuck the dummy a good way off, *not* in the direction of the gun of course. Send the puppy and as he sees the dummy almost within his reach get your helper to fire the gun or pistol. The puppy may jerk to a stop and look slightly startled, whereupon you give him encouragement to go on and pick the dummy. When he has brought it back, give him some time to recover and then repeat the performance. He may be better or worse, but no matter. End up with an ordinary retrieve without gunfire to put his mind at ease and to finish with a success. Leave him a day or two and then continue from there. If you handle it right he will soon get used to it and complete his retrieves nicely.

The next step is to substitute a bird or rabbit for the dummy. Use a grouse, a partridge, a small hen pheasant or a smallish rabbit (not a pregnant doe, nor a baby rabbit). Pigeons are not a good 'first retrieve', nor are duck. Most dogs hate picking woodcock at first, but get very good at it.

Now he is about ready to go to his first shoot. If possible don't shoot

there yourself the first time. Let him stand right behind the line and act as 'long-stop', choosing a bird for him that has fallen stone dead and, if possible, one he has seen. Make him wait for a long time before he is allowed to pick it, then treat it like a dummy-retrieve, giving him every help you can, but seeing that whatever happens he picks it and gets it safely to your hand.

Once he has picked a carefully chosen bird or two, you can start getting him up into the line, when he will soon get used to guns being fired over his head, now he knows what it is all about. From now on it is carefulness on your part in taking him gradually on for the first season and the start of the second season that counts, letting him gain experience all the time, but not rushing him and remembering to take him back a step or two if things go wrong.

Let him end every stint he does on a success. This will keep him keen and happy, until his first season is successfully over, when he should be on the way to being a useful shooting dog and have the makings of a Field Trialler.

Field Trials

Field Trials are run as a day's shooting in this country. A few Trials may take place on grouse in Scotland and the North of England in August, and some more on partridges in the South in September. However, the main Trial season for Retrievers starts on the first of

A Labrador should swim like an otter. Ch. Bumblikite of Mansergh retrieving from water (*left*). Mrs Ruth Tenison's F. T. Ch. Ballyfrema Lou going into water off a high bank (*right*).

October, when they come thick and fast until the beginning of December, when the Championship Stake is held to find the 'Winner of Winners,' the coveted grand finale of the hectic season. After that there are occasional Novice and Amateur Handler's Stakes, but the season is really over when the Championship is decided in December, as all the Open Stakes are run prior to the Championship.

Trials contain a large element of luck but if your puppy has gone well and is absolutely steady, retrieves nicely, has a good nose, style and speed, and will retrieve from water, it is fun to enter him in a Novice Stake and see how he goes on.

If you have joined one of the Labrador Clubs you may have had an opportunity to run him first in one of the Summer Working Tests on dummies. These put into practice all he has already learned in his training. They are very good practice for Trials, but you will find that proper Field Trials on live game are more difficult, allowing the dog very much more scope and initiative. There is an air of excitement in Field Trials too, that is not present in artificial Working Tests even if run on cold game, although dummies are the most usual retrieve in these Summer Tests.

The early stakes, in late September and early October, are nearly always 'walking-up' in roots, i.e. there is a long line consisting of three or four judges and either four or six dogs. I am going to describe a three-judge one-day stake. (Many of the big stakes, however, have four judges and a referee, and last for two days.)

A three-judge stake

The three judges each take station in the line, one on the right, one in the centre and one on the left. Each judge has a gun and a dog on each side of him, the *lower* number on the right of the line. So the right-hand judge takes dogs 1 and 2, the centre 3 and 4, the left-hand 5 and 6. The rest of the dogs remain on their leads with their handlers amongst the spectators who are clustered near a man with a flag, where they must stay to avoid getting in the way or being shot.

The line also has beaters, number-board carriers, stewards and the gamekeeper in charge, called the Steward of the Beat. At first each judge works alone, taking the game shot by 'his' two guns and sending the dogs in strict turn. When he has tested his first two dogs to his satisfaction, they return *on their leads* to the spectator's flag, and the next two come in. The Trials continue until all dogs have run under *two* of the three judges.

After that, the card is sorted by the judges according to their books, and in the afternoon, only dogs that are in the running are called, the others being allowed to go home if they wish.

Gradually the finalists are sorted, and the day usually ends with a 'run-off' for the one or two placings which may be very close. These finalists will be seen by all three judges, although two judges are sufficient, and eventually the Trial will end and the awards be announced. These consist of three Prizes, a Reserve, and one or two Certificates of Merit for dogs who have run well, but have not received prizes. The reserve dog gets a Certificate of Merit too.

The disqualifying sins are: (1) unsteadiness (i.e. 'running-in'); (2) hard mouth; (3) whining or barking in the line; (4) being out of control; (5) failure to enter water on command. These are all absolute disqualifications, so don't waste your money entering trials if you *know* your dog will fail in one of these. There is no redress; your dog will be *out* and your considerable entry-money gone down the drain. But if he is pretty certain not to make any of these mistakes, then take a chance and see how you get on.

To run successfully in Trials, the dog must be able to take help from the handler, because a lot of the birds he will be sent for will be unmarked, and he will have to be directed to the vicinity of the bird.

Being a shooting day, and the guns being guests of the kind host who has lent the ground, the dogs must not waste either their or the judges' time, so the dog must be able to get to the spot without undue delay and without annoying host and keeper by flushing a lot of unshot birds and disturbing a lot of unnecessary ground. If he does this he will soon be adjudged 'out of control' and will be scrapped.

Signals
By the use of diversion-dummy training (as I have described) he will have learned to follow general hand signals. He must also learn to stop and look for directions when the whistle is blown. The usual signals are: one pip, 'Look at me'; one long blast, 'Stop'; a chain of pips, 'Come back to me'. If he goes out in the wrong direction, pip once to stop him so that he looks at you, give him a hand signal, and if he again goes wrong pip again and give a further hand signal. When he sees the hare jump up, give him that long commanding blast that means 'Stop! Don't you dare!' and when the judge, disgusted that between you you have failed to find the bird, says 'Call him up', then give the chain of pips to tell him to stop hunting and come back to you. We also use a long 'falling' blast on the whistle which means 'Sit'. If you want to drop him at a distance, it is a most useful signal.

These whistle and hand signals will be needed if you run in Trials, but do try and handle as quietly as you can, only using the whistle if strictly necessary (try not to use it at all at a private shoot, because the host and the keepers hate it so much as a rule that they may never ask a noisy handler again).

Just as judges in the show ring sometimes forget that their one and only task is to place the dogs in their order of merit, so Field Triallers sometimes forget that their most important task is to get the bird. That is what the judges want, and if you fail then there will be a dog and handler only too eager to have a go with a possible chance of 'wiping your eye', the term used when one dog fails and the next picks up the bird he has been looking for. So in Trials you must really want to get that bird. Use every means in your power, moving to left or to right of your stance if necessary to get the wind right for your dog. And don't give up trying for the bird until the judge calls you up. Many a handler has become deaf just for a few seconds, if he thinks his dog is near the bird or just about to turn towards it. The judge will jolly soon stop you if he thinks you are going forward too far.

But with this encouragement I will pass on what an old handler said to me when I was a beginner: if at any time during a Trial I thought I was doing harm to a young dog, especially a puppy, I should take it out of the Trial rather than ruin it. I did this once, when a puppy of mine suddenly started to whine, a horrible trick which must be stopped without delay.

The puppy was doing extremely well that day and a lot of people thought I was mad to go out, but I got the puppy stopped at home, and he made a good dog. He would have been incurable had I continued to run him that day.

Once you have run in a stake you will have learned more about Trials and dogs and handling than I can ever tell you. Above all else, it needs experience to become really successful at Trials. Having made a reasonable job of your puppy, have a go and see how he goes on in a Novice or Puppy Stake. You will both love and hate every minute of it and will probably be frightened as you have never been before, but the 'bug' will bite you and you will probably never stop until you are so old that you can no longer plod through those 70-acre fields of dripping roots with a harum-scarum youngster that is about to go at the first pheasant that drops, thus in a trice losing you both your entry money and your nerve.

11 Labradors Abroad

The Labrador is not only one of the most popular breeds in Great Britain, but also in Ireland which has splendid Labradors and top-class breeders, running the most excellent Shows of all types, which many English breeders visit; there are also some very good Field Trials. I am always very impressed with the Irish Trial dogs when I go over; they have tremendous courage, style and drive, fear neither terribly thick covert nor bitterly cold water, and are absolutely in their element in mud that would stop English dogs in their tracks.

The Irish are great breeders of livestock, and although very many of their bloodlines go back to English or Scottish strains (notably the Blaircourts, the Sandylands and all the earlier English strains), they can breed excellent dogs in both spheres off their own bat. A tremendous number of good dogs came from both Mrs Eustace Duckett's wonderful dual-purpose Castlemore Kennel, and also from the Strokestown Labradors bred by Major and Mrs Pakenham Mahon, who also excelled in dogs able to win in both the Field and Championship shows. Another man to whom the working side owes a tremendous amount over the years is Jim Cranston, who has trained and handled many of the good F.T. Champions which have done such credit to the Irish reputation as great dog-men and breeders.

A beautiful Yellow dog from Ireland. Irish Ch. Kirklands Goldfinch.

A wonderful Irish dual-purpose bitch, F. T. Ch. Ballyfrema Lou.

Two others we must not forget are Mr P. J. Martin of the famous Fanebank Kennels who has kept a strain of great merit going for so many years and who with Mr Jim Haffey has come over to the English Championship Shows through thick and thin, taking us on at our own game, giving us a great run for our money, and indeed often showing us clean heels at such shows as Cruft's. Jim Haffey gained the dog Challenge Certificate and Best of Breed in 1971 with Int. Ch. Kinky of Keithray, bred by Mr and Mrs Wilkinson.

While the Irish have breeders and competitors like these they have nothing to fear from competition anywhere.

America
America has always been a great stronghold of the Labrador, although their Standard differs slightly from ours, in that they like a much bigger dog than we usually produce; only our more upstanding specimens meeting their Standard of height. They also call for rather less 'stop' than we do, thereby slightly altering the head and expression. The American Labradors are great dual-purpose dogs. Such kennels as the Ardens produce many Dual and F.T.Ch.s, and appear behind many of their best American-bred dogs today. Britain has also played her part in America recently, and their record show-winning dog, Int. Ch. Sam of Blaircourt, sent out by Gwen Broadley to Mrs Grace Lambert, has set a tremendous standard of wins that will take some beating.

One of the most famous American bitches Int. Ch. Kimvalley Picklewitch, twice supreme champion of the 'National', the most important Labrador show in America.

Like our Irish friends we have many American breeders who come over to our shows and we love to see them. Jim and Helen Warwick of the Lockerbie Labradors are so much part of the English summer show season, that we should be amazed if they were not there, sometimes as spectators, sometimes judging, and occasionally handling. Elizabeth Clark is also part and parcel of the English scene, and back in America, in partnership with the famous Labrador breeder Mrs Diana Beckett of Kimvalley fame, she has one of the strongest establishments, 'Springfields' Champion Labradors, which would be outside our wildest dreams in Britain. We must not forget Mrs Dorothy Howe of the Rupert Kennels, who has done a lot for American Labradors including writing a wonderful book on the subject, as has Helen Warwick, author of one of the most exhaustive books on the breed in any country.

These sorts of breeders are responsible for the very high standard of American Labradors in both Ring and Field, and the breed will go on from strength to strength.

Scandinavia

The Labrador did not really flourish until after World War II in the Scandinavian countries, but when the breed did get started out there, the Swedes, Norwegians, and Danes came over and looked and learned, as is their habit, being the most thorough people in anything they take up.

A good liver bitch in Sweden. Mrs Brit-Marie Brulin's Int. Ch. Puhs Chocolate Beauty.

They imported wisely and widely, and before long they were away with ever-improving standards. They are all so keen that it really is difficult to pin down specific breeders, because all of them are striving for the very best. Undoubtedly Mrs Brit-Marie Brulin of the Puhs Kennels has done a tremendous amount to stabilise the breed into its present high standard, both at Shows and in the Field; out there it seems to be the rule rather than the exception to work the Show Labradors. So Field Trials flourish, and with breeders like the Brulins, the Thoors (Mrs E-Son Thoor wrote an excellent book in Swedish on the breed, with wonderful photos and a wealth of useful information), the breed also flourishes. The Scandinavian judges are excellent too, and many of their great all-rounders come over and judge at Championship level here every summer.

The Danish Labradors, as in all these true working-dog countries, are excellent in each sphere. Baron Juel Brockdorff has made tremendous efforts to get the breed on the map in Denmark. When judging their Trials I was most impressed with the flair and determination with which their dogs hunted. They reminded me of the Irish dogs in this way, having the same faith that if they hunt hard enough the bird will be there. I was to find the same thing in Kenya when I judged Trials there. I believe this tremendous faith that a bird is down stems from their Trial dogs being actual shooting dogs in 'real life', handled by excellent shots. If the gun goes off and the handler sends the dog, then it is because there is a bird down. They never get stultified with eternal repetition in bare fields of the stop-and-go methods practised so endlessly at home by English Trial handlers and

An International Champion in Sweden, Int. Ch. Black Eagle of Mansergh, one of their leading sires.

trainers, and which produce either a brilliant dog, an automaton, or a dog that has got sickened by a surfeit of this type of practice work and has become 'stuck up'. Perhaps the main influences in Scandinavia have been the Sandylands Kennels, the Liddlys, the Cookridges and the Manserghs. A great dog out there is Scan. Dual Ch. Powhatan Sentry, the 'Golden Dog' as they call their Dog of the Year, who was sent out by the Aikenheads, and will be a great influence on future generations.

Africa

South Africa and Kenya have extremely keen Labrador breeders and strong clubs, both countries running Shows and Trials, as does Zimbabwe-Rhodesia. In South Africa, 'Hussar' and 'Brigade' are famous names, while the Cannobie Lee Kennels have a long line of

Mrs Gunilla Eks's black dog Grock of Mansergh in Sweden.

Champions to their credit, and Mr Douglas Goff has a strong kennel in Cape Province. Major Oscar Wilde is a keen and successful breeder of dual-purpose Labradors.

The Beadles Kennels had a great influence in South Africa, until the Jenkins moved back to England, where they still flourish in Herefordshire. They were based on the Heatheredge Kennels of Miss Margaret Ward in Yorkshire, and are concerned both with work and show.

Kenya is getting very keen indeed and I shall long remember the excellent Trial I was lucky enough to judge and which was held at Ontulele Farm on the slopes of Mt Kenya, on guinea fowl and yellow-necked francolin. Those dogs are like the Irish; they hunt and hunt in the worst of prickly scrub and dangerous going. They are true working dogs and fear nothing.

One of the main kennels for work and show is that of our Trial host and hostess, Mr and Mrs Robin Davis at Ontulele, Nanyuki. They have a very strong hand, based quite a lot on Irish and Scottish blood. These are true dual-purpose Labradors, ready either to shoot or go down to a show, whichever happens to be on the day's programme. Another big influence in Kenya was the Lonnachsloy Kennel, really a Scottish kennel because the Macfarlanes, after showing for many years in Britain, took their kennel out to Nairobi when they moved to a job out there, including that Grand Old Man 'Kenyan Ch. Dugald Dubh of Lonnachsloy'. This Scottish-bred black dog from a Blaircourt sire and dam has had a big influence out there and has stamped his stock as true Labradors. The Macfarlanes and Lonnachsloys have now left Kenya for America, and of course dear old Dugald Dubh is no more, though he lived to a very ripe old age. His tremendous influence for the true type and character will remain for many years to come in Kenya.

At the time I was out there, there was a good Dual Champion, I believe the first bred in Kenya, Dual Ch. General of Kaisuga, bred, owned and handled by Mr Charles Allardice, who at that time was in charge of the Police Dog Section. This dog will probably be in England by now, and a very charming clever dog he is.

Mr and Mrs Douglas Taylor in Kenya are also great names in Labradors, and over many years have done tremendously good work in fostering the dual-purpose Labrador in Kenya, having had some high class Champions themselves.

Australasia

Australia is another tremendous Labrador stronghold, running the most wonderful shows, importing a lot of top-quality dogs and working them too. Famous breeders are Mrs Pope, Mrs Gilbert of the Jaywick Kennels, the Dufton Labrador Champions, and many other keen breeders and well-known kennels of Champions. A big influence

Mr and Mrs Watts's Poolstead Perfectos, a winner of many awards both at Field Trials and in the show ring in New Zealand.

at the present time resulted from the importation into Australia of Aust. Ch. Sandylands Tan, that great British sire, who, mated to Sandylands Shadow, produced over a dozen Champions for the breeder Mrs Broadley, and many others. Recently Mrs Pope was over in England searching for an outcross for Tan bitches. She has had a great dog out there in Australian Ch. Ballyduff Cetus, bred by Mrs Docking, and was lucky enough to find a replica of this good dog at Miss Ryder's Redvales Kennel in Yorkshire, which was not only exactly like Cetus in looks but extremely closely related to him.

I have here only touched upon the surface of the subject of the many good breeders and keen dual-purpose enthusiasts overseas. Wherever Labradors are found there are keen breeders doing their utmost to keep the breed up to the high standard that has always been traditional in Labradors, from their beginning.

12 Labrador Tales

The Labrador has always been known as a great character, since the early days of the fishing dog with the white foot told in Chapter 5.

Whether they are blessed with great brains is more open to doubt; perhaps it is better that they shouldn't be the cleverest breed in the world, because the shooting dog that starts thinking for himself can be very difficult (especially if he has more brains than his master).

There are scores of amusing, extraordinary, sad and clever tales of the breed, and the stories I am going to tell here may give you an insight into the character of the Labradors concerned, possibly even their psychology, not to speak of those of their owners in one or two tales. Some are of my own dogs, because in a long life in Labradors I have had many different dogs who varied enormously in thinking power, humour and character.

Probably the soundest and certainly the cleverest Labrador I ever owned – Eastview Black Prince of Mansergh at eight months.

I will start, however, with a great dog in every way, who caused a lot of amusement whatever he did, and was much loved and respected by all who knew him, Dual Champion Knaith Banjo. He belonged to his breeder (or was it the other way round?) Mrs Veronica Wormald, who with her husband, Major Arthur Wormald, did so much for the dual-purpose yellow Labrador, being one of the very earliest yellow breeders.

Her great Banjo was at his prime in the years following World War II when Trials were starting again; he ran for about 8 years, and won at least 37 Awards, being one of the ten Dual Champions in the breed.

He was known as the dog that never wasted a moment, but improved the shining hour whatever he was doing. If he was in the line at a Trial, he watched every bird all day, and when he came out of the line he wasted not a second but set about the bitches waiting to go in. I well remember one boring Trial on a hot day with no scent, with no birds and hours of waiting for nothing to come to the guns. The beaters were driving in an enormous tract of the Yorkshire Wolds with not a thing stirring, and guns, judges, handlers, and dogs were virtually asleep in the noonday sun. I looked down the line at the curled-up sleeping dogs, but there was one at attention. Banjo was sitting up watching every move with his ears at the ready just in case something should come. That was the character of this dog and he was the same with hunting. When he hunted he hunted, and he didn't stop till he found something.

The episode by which I shall best remember Banjo took place in the Northumberland and Durham Open Stake at Lambton Castle. We were standing in the deep bottom of a very steep ghyll on the river bank. Where we were standing there was a tremendously high, absolutely sheer bank where the cliff had broken clean away leaving a sharp edge at the summit. The beaters were driving the pheasants over the river from the top of this cliff, which had high beech trees, so the birds were real scorchers.

I was in the line with my foundation bitch Carry of Mansergh, and Mrs Wormald with Banjo, ('Jo', as she called him). Our gun was Sir 'Copper' Blackett, and below us was Lord Lambton himself.

Suddenly, off the top of the bank over the beech trees, came three cock pheasants, really high birds, and with them a huge Rhode Island Red barn-yard cock. They came off the high bank in line over the trees, like horses coming abreast over Bechers. It is the only time I have seen three dead pheasants in the air at tree-top height at the same moment, because Lord Lambton got a right and left, and Copper Blackett killed his at the same moment. The rooster, who must have been astonished to find himself at that height anyhow, saw his companions plummet to earth, so came too, and all four landed with a fearful thump into the masses of scrub, bushes, wild rhubarb and willow herb that covered a sandy spit or island in the middle of the little river. The drive now being over, the other judge sent his two dogs first, and very quickly each returned with a dead pheasant. Then it was my turn, and Carry crossed the water and plunged into the scrub, rapidly returning with her bird, the third pheasant. To our astonishment, the judge said to Mrs Wormald, 'Send your dog', and when we looked surprised he insisted there was another pheasant down, 'a dead cock'. We tried to tell him that all the birds were picked, but competitors must not argue with judges who have 'seen the bird down with his own eyes'. Banjo was duly sent. He worked hard and well, found, acknowledged, and rightly left all three 'falls' where we had picked our birds and eventually having completely combed every inch of land, bushes, and water came out and looked at his handler. She sent him back and he hunted every inch again, only to come back again empty-handed to be sent again. He tried hard, but of course there was no pheasant to pick. Again we made a half-hearted protest but the judge was adamant. 'There was a cock down', he said. How right he was. Banjo, when told to go again, turned with a comical look of disgust on his face, lifted his leg meaningfully against the nearest willow-bush, strolled very slowly and stiff-legged into the edge of the scrub, and picked up the cowering rooster from his hidey-hole, where he had been crouching motionless while Banjo had been hunting all round him. Banjo had known perfectly well he was there, and indeed exactly where he was, because he did not have to hunt for the cock, just stroll stiff-legged in protest and pick him up. He carried the purple-faced rooster out very slowly and delivered him to Mrs Wormald's hand, making sure he passed the judge on the way, – indeed making a detour especially to do so. I thought for one glorious moment he was going to lift his leg against the judge, but he was too much of a gentleman (although he definitely thought of doing so). He had delivered the goods and that was the end of the matter. 'Whatever was *that* doing there,' said the judge, and then, hearing the hens squawking on top of the cliff, he looked up, turned rather pink and moved away.

Of all my Labradors, every one of whom descends from Carry, the cleverest by far were Eastview Black Prince of Mansergh and his descendants. 'Timmy', as we called Black Prince, was by my old Ch. Midnight out of a bitch descending from Heatheredge Caprice, brother to Ch. Careena of H. He had Mc Ginn's Favourite in his pedigree, who was, I think, the cleverest Trial and Shooting dog I have ever seen. Timmy himself was outstanding for brain, and was one of the most

difficult dogs that I have ever had, simply because of this. I loved him
dearly, but knew that if I wasn't on my toes Timmy would anticipate a
situation and act on it without delay, having thought it out and found a
solution in a flash. I remember him, when working on Lord
Shuttleworth's shoot at Leck, putting up a wounded hen pheasant that
he had been sent for and that could still fly. This hen glided down over
the young larches and across the Leck Beck, landing high in the
branches of an ash tree. Timmy very nearly caught her as she got up
but the steep bank down caused him just to miss her, so he tore down
through the larches after her. I knew she would never get up again and
that she would eventually fall dead out of the tree, so started down after
them. I didn't need to go down far because Timmy had the situation
well in hand. He stood on the river bank and sized up the situation.
That is where he differed from any other dog I have had; he made his
plan like a General, put it into action, and it worked first time.

To the fascination of those watching, he ran upstream till he could
jump the wire fence down into the river. He crossed, and climbed out
the other side twenty yards above the tree, where he could get up the
bank. He ran down the field and looked at the bird, saw he couldn't
offer to reach it, and so didn't try, but turned back upstream again
until he could get on top of a broken wall that ran underneath the tree.
Once on the wall he ran along the top until directly under the bird,
when he launched himself, seized a branch just below the bird, and
hung on by his teeth. Of course he swung out into space with his own
launching-impetus, which shook the branches, and the bird was
knocked out and landed in the river just after Timmy did, and quite
near him. He swept her up before she could gather her wits, took her
upstream to where he could cross again, then jumped the wire fence,
and brought the bird triumphantly back to hand.

Timmy was a dog that I have no doubt could work out a problem
mentally, with the rudiments of an intellect, which most dogs don't
have in any shape or form. He could foresee the problems and work
them out in his head without recourse to trial and error. He was also a
great comic, and I remember one extremely cold winter's day when the
boys from Sedbergh School were up skating on the Lake. We had taken
all the Labradors and Terriers for a walk across the moor at sunset, and
were well away from home when Timmy, who had been 'absent
without leave', suddenly joined us from the direction of the Lake
bearing a pair of trousers, complete with braces. To our horror they
were still warm, and we pictured some wretched boy cowering behind a
rhododendron bush shaking with cold in his underpants, his trousers
having mysteriously vanished without trace. What that poor chap did
we never knew. We hung them on a bush near the Lake. Next morning
they had gone. I knew perfectly well from Timmy's face that he knew

it was funny and was enjoying the cruel joke as much as we were.

My old Cora, in her old age, learned to laugh. I don't mean smile with wreathed lips, as many Labradors do. She laughed out loud. She proved to me, too, that a dog can remember an incident in detail perfectly clearly for a full year. It was autumn, and the gutters at Lilymere were full of dead leaves. I got out an old wooden ladder and proceeded up it to the gutter on the house opposite the dog kennels. The dogs all watched intently, and I was half way up when a rung broke, and the momentum of the fall broke the next two or three, leaving me hanging by my hands in the good old pantomime fashion. Cora gave a great guffaw of laughter, out loud with open mouth, nearly choking herself with laughter; it was the first time I had heard or seen a dog do this. After that first outburst, she would often guffaw out loud if anything tickled her fancy, such as when one puppy chased our cock bantam till it flew into the mouth of another puppy, or when one day a furious rabbit chased my old Ch. Midnight right down the garden path. But to prove she remembered the ladder incident, about a year later, when the gutters were again filled with autumn leaves, I asked the house-painter to clear the gutter for me in the same place. He set his ladder against the self-same wall, and as he put his foot on the first rung, Cora looked at me and laughed out loud. That shook me to the core, because before that I had thought that dogs had only the dimmest recollection of past events and no idea at all of anticipating the possible result of an action either by memory or implication. She was not a particularly brainy bitch either, but she remembered.

An amusing incident happened in a field of tall kale at one of the northern Trials. A handler was walking in line, actually in the Open Stake, when he glanced down at his heel and to his horror saw that his dog had gone. Keeping his head admirably, he walked on as though nothing had happened, saying at intervals, 'Heel, good dog', just as though the dog was there. A cock pheasant got up in front and was shot dead quite a long way out. 'Send your dog', said the judge, whereupon the handler said, 'Hie lost', and then proceeded to give a great display of handling, stopping his 'dog' on the whistle, and waving him hither and thither on to the bird. Of course, the 'dog' did not come back with it and handler and judge were deciding it must have run, 'because he has hunted out every inch of where it fell', when the handler to his great relief saw the dog arriving up from behind with a pheasant. Where he had got it from and what he'd been doing and when he had decided to take French leave, we shall never know, but the handler heeled the correct bird in, when they eventually walked over it. That quick-witted handler really deserved to win, for resource and initiative alone.

One extraordinary event that happened in Labradors was the advent of the bitch that became known as 'Mrs Wormald's Chow', registered as Knaith Stanleywood Spot.

What happened was that a black bitch visited Knaith Bandboy (Banjo's son) and duly, to the day, produced a litter of puppies for her breeder at Ormskirk. The puppies, at 8 weeks, went to their new homes, Mrs Wormald going down and picking one for herself. They all grew into very handsome puppies, but one day, while they were still very young, Mrs Wormald rang me up to ask whether, when getting Yellow bitches to my Black stud dogs, the resulting Yellow puppies ever had a black spot on their tongues? I said that I had seen it occasionally, whereupon Mrs Wormald told me that this puppy of hers, by Bandboy out of the black Ormskirk bitch, had a biggish spot on her tongue. In due course, she sent the puppy to Jack Chudley to be trained, and after he had had it some time Jack rang up and said that it was a funny bitch to train and sometimes did well and sometimes turned a bit odd in its work, and that he wasn't sure that Mrs Wormald would like it, and should he go on with it? Mrs Wormald was very keen to have this bitch for Trials and shows, it being the last she had of Bandboy's puppies. So she told Jack to go on with it.

Meanwhile this litter had reached the age of six months and more, and one of them was shown by a novice at St Helen's show. Mr Tom Dinwoodie, one of our best Labrador judges, was judging and he asked the Steward what a Chow was doing in the Labrador class, and would the Steward send it out. The Steward agreed that it had a Chowish look about it, but said it was entered as a Labrador, and actually was a Labrador with a Labrador's pedigree given in the Catalogue, all correct. Tom replied that he knew a Chow when he saw it, and a slight problem arose, the wretched novice being horrified to be told that his precious puppy that he had reared so well was half a Chow. I never did hear how this got sorted out, but shortly after this Mrs Wormald got her bitch back from the Chudleys. To her horror the whole mouth, tongue, lips and gums had turned the blackish-blue of a Chow. Gradually the realisation came that another dog had mated the black bitch just before she was mated to Bandboy, and that the puppies *were* half-bred; on enquiry a Chow was found to live about half a mile down the lane from the bitch. So everyone, breeder, Mrs Wormald, the unfortunate novice, and all the other purchasers, got their heads together and sent the whole affair up to the Kennel Club as a genuine mistake, and asked the K.C. to annul the Registrations and all the papers. To their astonishment, the Kennel Club refused to do this, probably quite rightly, because they had proof from Mrs Wormald and the Breeder that the bitch *had* actually been mated to Bandboy, and had no proof whatsoever that any other dog had mated her. So the Kennel Club apparently felt that after all that time with no real evidence to prove otherwise, the original Registrations must stand.

'Right,' said Mrs Wormald, who herself was undoubtedly the greatest character we have ever had in Labradors, 'I'm going to get this bitch into the K.C. Stud Book both as a bench winner and as a Field Trial Winner, and the Kennel Club will know for evermore, because I've already told them, that they have a half-bred Labrador–Chow in their precious Stud Book'. So she set about it, and succeeded in wiping my eye on a hare at the Penrith Trials, with her 'Chow' getting a Certificate of Merit, and thus winning Spot's way into the Stud book as a Trial winner, as she had threatened the Kennel Club that she would.

To get her in as a Championship Show Winner wasn't quite so easy, because you had only to see her blue-black tongue and gums to discard her on sight.

The great day so nearly came at the Northumberland and Durham Labrador Club Championship show with Mr Fred Wrigley judging. To Mrs Wormald's great joy, there were only four dogs entered in the Field Trial Class, a class which gives automatic entry to the Stud Book if you win First, Second or Third prize. By the time it came to the class at the end of the day Mr Wrigley was tired and had got into his automatic judging routine of examining the ears, head, and eye and then opening the mouth to see the teeth. After some hundred or two of pink mouths it must have been an almighty shock to open Spot's mouth and see that sinister blue-black cavern. He leaped back, rubbing his hands on his trousers as though he had touched a snake by mistake, exclaiming 'Not the Chow!' 'Yes, Fred,' replied Mrs Wormald.' What are you going to do about it?' 'I'm going to put you there, Madam', said Mr Wrigley, pointing to the bottom of the Class. She had missed the coveted stud-book entry by one place. But her promise to the Kennel Club was half fulfilled and Spot is 'in the Book' as a Trial winner, where she remains immortal to this day. Afterwards Spot was given to Mrs Wormald's son in Yorkshire, but she used to bring her out at a show again occasionally, especially under me, after Spot had been forgotten for a while, just for the pleasure of making us judges jump out of our skins.

Spot lived to a ripe and honourable old age, being a charming bitch much loved by the family and the grandchildren and a great credit both to her Labrador ancestry and to her Chow parentage.

A dear old Yellow dog, belonging to Mr John Hirst, was a great character. He came to us to train at Lilymere as a youngish puppy, and was without exception the largest Labrador I have ever set eyes on. I have to this day, a garage wall where we measured our Labradors at the shoulder to see that we were keeping more or less to the standard, which ranges from 21½ in. to 22½ in., this covering both dogs and bitches. If we had a really large one to measure or a really small one we marked the shoulder height on the white wall against which they stood.

Reanacre Sandylands Tarmac was our own largest dog, standing 23¾ in., which stopped him from gaining his title. He really *was* too big, as I found out shooting. Plenty of people would give *me* a lift up to the butts in their Land Rover, but no one would have Tarmac, so we had to walk. But he was a midget compared with Copper. Copper tipped him at the shoulder by three inches.

When young, poor old Copper's brain did not keep time with his rate of growth, and he took a long time to grasp the idea of retrieving. I could not get him to retrieve. If he was on a check cord he would find the end of his own cord and bring 'himself' to me with great pride, and if not on a check cord, he would wander off to the fir-trees to gather a fir-cone, and at that stage he stuck. However one day he grasped the idea and started retrieving dummies. I was delighted, and worked with him secretly for some days. When I was absolutely sure he knew what he was doing and enjoyed it, I told my husband that I had 'got Copper going' at which he showed blank disbelief and said he'd only believe that when he saw it with his own eyes.

So telling my husband to stand well back to one side and to keep quiet so as not to disturb Copper's concentration, I hurled the dummy up the bank into the bushes. Copper watched it with a most intelligent expression and when I said 'Hie lost', set off with great elan. He did a quick detour round, seized my husband by the back of his breeches and propelled him to me at top speed.

Dear old Copper! He made a good old dog in the end, and shot in Norfolk till the end of his days, having most acute hearing, so that he proved invaluable when duck-flighting or pigeon-shooting in the dusk. He could hear the slightest whisper of wings, and would turn his head to them telling his owner exactly when and where the birds were coming. This was a tremendous asset, and he was much missed when his time came to go. It's sad when old dogs die, but the shooting man has to get on with the next, and I'm glad to say that an extremely nice bitch took over Copper's job and was a most successful shooting-bitch for many years.

The prodigious greed of the Labrador breed is legendary, but who can beat my Ch. Midnight, whom I saw carrying a completely empty 2-lb glass jam jar in his mouth? He was only a Junior still, although it was the morning of a Trial for him, so I hastily rushed out of the back door to get it from him. This was the worst thing I could have done, because he gave one enormous crunch and swallowed the lot. I dashed back to my husband and told him what had happened, but all he said was that he'd boiled a whole rabbit with its skin on for the dogs the night before and that I must give Middy the skin and then go on to the Trial with him. Middy wolfed the skin with the same alacrity with which he had swallowed the huge pieces of broken glass, and that was the end of that. We never saw a sign of that jam jar again, and he did twelve and a half shooting seasons, so it couldn't have done him much harm.

And what about these huntin'-shootin'-fishin' old Labradors, nearly always Black, who would belong to the local Conservative Club if given half a chance?

Major and Mrs Jimmy Gaddum of Burneside in Westmorland had just such a dog. At the time they had a very nice girl staying with them called Molly. She was just about to buy herself a new suit and being rather a smart person she daringly decided (with the great approval of the Gaddums, who egged her on) to buy a trouser suit at a time when trousers had only just come into fashion. One day after hunting, a few people came in for drinks and Molly went upstairs to bath and change into dry clothes. She put on the trousers for the first time, and amid great applause from the guests, she made her entrance. The old dog took one horrified look, ascended the stairs to her bedroom, and came down bearing her skirt in his mouth, which he handed to her, very clearly showing his disapproval of such outrageous goings on.

By now I must have given an idea of the different characters of Labradors I have met and admired, but I will finish this book with what is perhaps the best summing up of a Labrador since the great dictum of the old days, that the salient points of a Labrador were 'expression, coat and tail'.

The modern version was given to my sister, who had been talking to a top-brass policeman, the head of the whole of a big police dog section in the London area. My sister remarked that she had noticed on television that in a recent high-security operation with aircraft hijacking, only Alsatians had appeared, no Labradors. The Top Brass said that Labradors were not suitable for the particular job they had to deal with that day on the aerodrome, but agreed that he did have quite a lot of Labradors in his force. My sister asked what job they did best. His reply was succinct: 'Narcotics, explosives and human remains.'

Appendix

The Kennel Club

The Kennel Club's address: 1 Clarges Street, Piccadilly, London W1Y 8AB. Telephone number: 01-493 6651.

Registration forms, Transfer Forms, Export Pedigrees, Change of Name Forms, and Kennel Club Standards of the Breeds etc., can be obtained direct from the above address. The various official forms are free, the K.C. Standards can be obtained for a small amount. The Kennel Club is the ultimate authority in dogs, publishing the annual *Kennel Club Stud Books* which are the only official records of all major wins. They run Cruft's Dog Show, and publish a monthly *Kennel Gazette* containing important official news such as Breed Records of all Registrations, notices of Championship judging appointments, new Rules and Regulations, a list of Shows and Field Trials with dates and Secretaries' addresses, and all-important official Kennel Pronouncements. All objections and disqualifications are made to or by them. The much coveted Challenge Certificates which count towards the various titles of Champion are their property, and are allocated to the various Shows and Trials by them alone.

Everyone who signs a Registration form puts themselves under the Jurisdiction of the Kennel Club, who may penalise any exhibitor or defaulter for their behaviour or malpractice; the penalties are often fines, and may include disqualification from attending or taking part in any Show or Field Trial under the Club's jurisdiction, perhaps for life.

Titles

The Title of Champion (Ch.) is gained by winning three Kennel Club Challenge Certificates under three different judges at official Championship Shows. In the case of gun dogs, before the full title of Champion may be obtained, the dog must qualify in the Field at an official Field Trial or Qualifying Day held under Kennel Club rules. Until then it may only assume the title of Show Champion (Sh. Ch.). The rules for gaining the title of Field Trial Champion (F.T.Ch.) differ in various breeds. For Labradors, the title is gained either by winning the Retrieve Championship Stake, or by winning two first prizes in two different stakes, one of which must be open to any breed of Retriever, and both of which stakes must be Open or All-Age stakes.

Before a Labrador can be described as F.T.Ch., it must have proved to have sat quietly in a drive, and passed a water test. These two conditions must have been fulfilled at certain specified stakes.

Dual Ch. is the unofficial title used for dogs that have become Champions on the show-bench and in Field Trials. The correct official title is actually Ch. and F. T. Ch., the aforesaid 'Dual Ch.' being a useful shortening of the correct title.

Obedience Ch. (Obed. Ch.) is gained by winning three Obedience Challenge Certificates under three different judges; or by winning the Obedience Challenge Certificate at Cruft's.

Show Gundog Working Certificates

To qualify a gun dog in the Field so that he may assume the full title of Champion, he must either win a Certificate of Merit or higher award at a recognised Field Trial held under Kennel Club rules, or gain a 'Show Gundog Working Certificate'.

In order to do this, the Labrador must be entered for its 'Qualifier' at a Field Trial where two of the judges at least must be on the 'A' judging-list. The dog must be off the lead in the line to prove he is not gun-shy. He must show that he will hunt and retrieve a bird tenderly to hand, to prove his natural instincts are there, and that he is not hard-mouthed. Steadiness is *not* essential, neither is water-work.

The dog must have won one Challenge Certificate on the bench before he is allowed to enter for a Show Gundog Working Certificate at actual Trials, but some Clubs run special days by Kennel Club permission where 'A' judges officiate in order to award Show Gundog Working Certificates. To enter one of these special Qualifying Days, the Labrador must have won a first prize at a Championship Show.

If he fails at either a Field Trial or a Qualifying Day, he cannot have more than two more attempts to qualify in his life and not more than twice in one shooting season.

Junior Warrant

A Junior Warrant is granted by the Kennel Club to a Labrador that has won 25 'points' at Championship or Open Shows *in breed classes* before it reaches the age of 18 months (variety classes do not count, even if for 'Any Variety Retrievers'). Points are as follows: Championship Shows, 3 points for each First Prize in a breed class. Open Shows, 1 point for each First Prize in a breed class.

At both Championship and Open Shows, First Prizes in Puppy and Minor Puppy Classes count towards the award of Junior Warrant which is *not* a title, so does *not* appear in front of the dog's name. It does, however, appear listed in the *Kennel Club Year Book*, although it is not recorded in the *Kennel Club Stud Book*.

Labrador Clubs

There are twelve Labrador Clubs in Britain at the time of writing (August 1979). The Clubs are as follows and the addresses of the Hon. Secretaries can be obtained from the Kennel Club, 1 Clarges Street, London W1.

The Labrador Retriever Club
The East Anglian Labrador Retriever Club
The Labrador Club of Scotland
The Labrador Retriever Club of Northern Ireland
The Midland Counties Labrador Retriever Club
The Northumberland and Durham Labrador Retriever Club
The North West Labrador Retriever Club
The Three Ridings Labrador Club
The West of England Labrador Retriever Club
The Labrador Retriever Club of Wales
The Yellow Labrador Club
The Kent, Surrey and Sussex Labrador Club

RECOMMENDED BOOKS ON LABRADORS

Clayton, Harold, *The 1972 & 1977 Labrador Books* (published privately)
Hill, F., Warner, *Labradors* (Foyles, 1961)
Howe, Dorothy, *This is the Labrador Retriever* (T. F. H. Publications Inc. U.S.A.)
Howe, Countess Lorna, *The Popular Labrador Retriever* (Popular Dogs)
Kinsella, Miriam, *Labradors* (Arthur Barker Ltd., 1972)
Moxon, P. R. A., *Gundogs Training and Field Trials (The Shooting Times)*
Roslin-Williams, Mary, *The Dual-Purpose Labrador* (Pelham Books Ltd., 1969)
Sanderson, Mackay, *Stud Book and Records of Field Trials* (Out of print and extremely rare)
Warwick, Helen, *The Complete Labrador Retriever* (Howell Book House, U.S.A.)

Index